MOLLY'S SECRET

When Molly helps a man to escape from an old mill where two Ebton villagers have left him trussed up, she unwittingly changes her own destiny, her family's and that of the village. Her secret, if discovered, would have her ostracised. The opportunity to leave her simple life behind comes when the handsome Lieutenant James Deadman professes his love for her, asking her to be his wife. However, his cousin, Dr Russell Deadman, seems determined to foil their match . . .

VALERIE HOLMES

MOLLY'S SECRET

Complete and Unabridged

LINFORD
Leicester

First published in Great Britain in 2010

First Linford Edition
published 2010

British Library CIP Data

Holmes, Valerie.
   Molly's secret.- -(Linford romance library)
   1. Love stories.
   2. Large type books.
   I. Title II. Series
   823.9′2–dc22

   ISBN 978–1–44480–339–6

Published by
F. A. Thorpe (Publishing)
Anstey, Leicestershire

Set by Words & Graphics Ltd.
Anstey, Leicestershire
Printed and bound in Great Britain by
T. J. International Ltd., Padstow, Cornwall

1

Sunshine filtered through the branches of the trees, dappling light playing with the colour and shape of the leaves. The spring had seemed an interminably long time coming as Molly rested her back against the old hut behind the inn, enjoying the relative peace of the place. She could hear the waves crashing on the beach the other side of the inn in the near distance, as the spring tides were high and bountiful.

The inn, along with a few fishermen's cottages and their boats, nestled along the shoreline of the beach in the sandy bay near the headland of Stangcliffe. It could be a violent, treacherous place when the weather was bad, but on a day like today it was, to Molly, a little haven away from her family's cottage behind the old church in the town of Ebton. Here the world moved and changed.

Her father had forbidden her to venture down the wooded gill to the old village, but since childhood it had been her secret place of discovery. The gill provided a place to hide, watch and keep secrets, because she knew things went on in there that were ignored by the townsfolk — a secret trade alongside the usual one of fishing.

She'd listened to old Amie, Amos's sister, tell her tales of hobgoblins, creatures that lived in caves in the headland. Amos owned the inn. Molly had even tried to find them, these mystical little creatures, but all she'd discovered was the wet, sandy places where men had stashed things and frightened the hobgoblins away. Molly had been a girl then. Now she was a young woman, but the child in her remained, refusing to leave her to settle to a life of chores and child-rearing.

She stood up and dusted her skirts down, wiping some of the sand from her boots on the edge of the rough grass before heading up the narrow track which would lead her back to her home. She didn't want to leave this place. However, she knew she had been there too long. Molly had intended to speak to Amie, but instead had been lost to daydreams as she watched the new growth and the creatures which signalled spring was here.

Her father would expect his dinner to be ready. She looked down at the selection of herbs in her basket, next to the eggs and cheese collected from the farm earlier in the day, and sighed. It would be a sorry meal for a man. Then she stopped and glanced back at the inn. I wonder, she whispered to herself as she turned back, perhaps Amie could help her out.

Molly placed her ear to the door of the inn. Amie was often in the back, taking her nap or swigging a drink of porter. Molly knew that there were a few fishermen in the inn already. Tentatively, she peered around the door, her cloth hat catching on a small splinter of wood. Molly put her basket down by her feet and concentrated on unhooking herself. Once free again, and having made sure that no damage had been done to her bonnet, she bent low to pick up her basket. There was an angry shout from inside the small building. Molly crouched down and inched intuitively behind two large barrels just inside the door.

Two men entered from the front room of the inn, roughly shoving a third into the small dark back room. Amie was nowhere to be seen. She'd hoped to ask Amie for some help with dinner, that was all, yet now she wished dearly she had gone home. The older woman was still working in the place and Molly saw her most Sundays over on the moor road as she walked back from church.

Molly was too embarrassed to stand up and admit she had snooped inside the inn, or risk word getting back to her father that she had entered this forbidden place. She thought she'd stay hidden just until the men left, then she would run home and serve her dad what she could muster for his simple dinner and hope he wouldn't be too cross or disappointed with her.

Her mother was away from home for a few days visiting Molly's aunt, Sarah, who lived in the market town of Gorebeck. Together they were making arrangements for Molly. That meant a husband was being found for her — a suitable match. Her sister Muriel had already been wed to a young lieutenant. They considered it a very good match. Molly did not. He would go to the wars and Muriel would be left to wonder and wait. He was too pompous for Molly anyway. He had connections with families who were far better than theirs, and had only settled for Muriel because his father had languished in debtors prison.

'Right, man, what have you been telling folk? Speak honestly or I shall beat it out of you.' Amos had hold of the stranger by the neck. Jeffries, a fisherman, had the man's arms pinned behind his back. He was quite tall,

5

strong looking, but no match for these two weather-beaten men who had spent their lives by or on the sea.

'Telling who, what?' the man asked calmly, looking straight at Amos.

'Cocky swab, aren't thee?' Amos balled his fist and punched the man in the stomach. His victim folded double. Jeffries was holding his arms preventing the stranger from falling to the ground.

Molly took in a sharp breath, so filled with fear, though, that she did not make a sound. She peered from her dark place between the two large barrels making sure her skirts were obscured from their view.

The man was pulled straight again.

'Now, pretty boy, you can tell me or the fishes, choice is yours . . . Who have you been telling about our business? We can take you out in a boat and you'd never be seen again,' Jeffries threatened, and pulled his arms high making the man groan with pain before he lowered them again.

'I came for a drink here. I was

passing through. Why should I be interested in your business?' The man glared at Amos who shrugged.

'You see that's why I don't believe thee. No one just passes here as we are off the main road by some miles. You have to be looking for us,' Jeffries growled in his ear.

'I was lost,' the man offered.

'Looks like we'll have to beat the truth out of you. See, we don't like strangers 'passing through', asking questions on their way. We'll give you something to remember us by, so you don't ask no more questions around here or lose your way again.' He looked at Jeffries. 'Take him to the old mill in the gill and tie him up sound. We'll sort him out later when the place is empty.'

Jeffries nodded. 'What about his horse?'

'Send it with Jeb to Ezekiel, he'll sell it on. The Revenue can fork out for another one. I can smell a revenue man a mile off — and you stink badly!' Jeffries swung his fist straight at the

7

stranger's temple, making him buckle at the knees. The man was released for a moment, obviously dazed, whilst Amos fetched a length of rope.

Molly stared at the injured man from behind her hiding place between the barrels. His eyes seemed to look in her direction without seeing at first. Then the bleariness cleared and she realised he was staring directly at her. She shrank back against the inn's wall, curled up and frightened.

Amos returned and Jeffries dragged the stranger to his feet. He mouthed two words, unmistakable in their plea, 'Help me'.

Molly froze, hardly daring to breathe. What if Jeffries or Amos saw her now? She'd be in a great deal of trouble for sure. Or, if her father knew she was here, in the forbidden village — in the inn, he'd take his cane to her. Either way, she had to get out unseen. But what of the stranger? He was in for a beating. He already had blood dripping down his cheek from his forehead as he was half dragged out of the inn.

She waited until the sound of the scuffle outside subsided. Amos came back to the room but did not look back, returning to the front of the inn. Unsteadily, Molly stood up; seeing the way was clear she ran up the path and into the gill. The wooded path which ran at the side of the river led her the same way as Jeffries was taking the man; she had to pass the old mill to climb up to the field that would lead her to her home.

Molly knew she had disobeyed her father. She had no business being there, but fate had decreed she now had no choice. She had to help the stranger and in so doing she would start a lot of trouble, but how much she had no idea.

2

Molly deliberately took an old track that would let her climb above the main path which followed the course of the narrow, fast flowing river. The banks were steep and the course cut the wooded gill in two. It was a wild, sheltered place, old as time, people said. It was also shrouded in superstition as things went on there and had done for years. No one trod those paths in the dark — well, not decent folk. Molly knew them well, but only in the daylight hours. Her track would lead her away from Jeffries and the stranger, who he carried, his reluctant load thrown across his broad shoulders. He'd threatened to shoot the man if he wriggled or tried to break free.

She overtook them and waited by the old fallen wall which surrounded the mill. Soon the two men emerged from the cover of the trees to disappear behind the overgrown walls of the mill. Jeffries pushed open the decrepit door and dropped the man down on the flagstone floor. Even from outside she heard the man groan as he landed. Jeffries had his pistol in his hand as he pushed his victim back with his foot. From where she was she could just see that they had tied his hands behind his back. Jeffries still carried a length of rope around his shoulder. He disappeared inside. Molly could not hear what was being said but could just make out shouting and what sounded like another blow — then silence.

A few moments later Jeffries reappeared. He rubbed his hands together as if pleased with a job well done, then shut the door behind him, wedging it with a piece of a broken branch. Quickly he made his way back through the woods. Molly counted to ten slowly, and then another five just in case she had been too quick with nerves, before stepping out into what had once been the yard in front of the mill. Now weeds pushed through between stones. She ran over to the door, dislodged the branch and, after taking a deep breath, pushed it open letting daylight flood the inside. Molly gasped as she saw the crumpled figure of the stranger tied hand and foot against the wall. He had a noose slipped around his neck. This had been secured to an iron ring on the wall. If he wriggled too much he could have hanged himself where he knelt. Molly dropped her basket and ran over to him. Whoever he was, he did not deserve this. No one did.

'Sir!'

His wide eyes stared imploringly at her. She loosed the rope around his neck. His eyes were wide, pleading. It would have been difficult for anyone not to show fear in such circumstances. As soon as his head was free he dropped forward and sighed deeply.

'Thank God you were there. Thank God you were brave enough to come. If I'd slipped I'd have choked to death.

Damn the blackguards! Untie me; we must get out of here.'

He was breathing heavily, his chest heaving as he regained his composure.

'Are you a revenue man?' Molly asked as she worked at untying the ropes.

'No, miss. Come with me, miss, and I shall make sure you are safe. You will never have to work in such a place again. I promise you, your past will be erased; it will not be spoken of. I will take you somewhere where you will be shown how to live like a lady and be treated as such. Your act of humanity towards me today will be rewarded. I shall be a friend to you. For saving my life, I will make sure you have one worth living.'

Molly was not really listening to him. She was intent on freeing the man and having both of them leave the area as soon as possible. She did not want to be seen there and he needed to be far away from Amos and Jeffries. She would take him home with her and ask her father what they should do to help him and sort out the two bullies at the inn. Finally the knots were undone and she helped him stand up on to his feet.

'Come,' he said, and swept up her basket in one hand and led her out holding her hand in his other.

She could not speak as they ran along. He seemed to know the way up to the moor road.

'Sir!' she said, but was ignored. 'Sir, I will take you to my home. My father will help you I am sure.'

He stopped momentarily. 'You have a father?'

'Of course, I do . . . '

'You worked in the inn and yet you have a father?' He was looking at her in a peculiar manner as if seeing her properly for the first time. He was appraising her dress.

'No! I mean, I shouldn't have been in there. I was looking for someone.'

'You have 'a friend' already within the village.' He nodded knowingly.

Molly pulled her hand from his. 'You

presume too much, sir. I was looking for old Amie. I should not have been in there it is true, but I was not having an assignation. However, it is just as well for you that I was where I should not have been, isn't it?'

'Yes, indeed it was. But who is your father?'

'My father is a retired sergeant from the 95th. He has served his country well but now has an injured arm. We own a cottage up there in the town and I should be home already. If you come with me I will explain to him that you are in danger and we can ask him for help. He will know what to do.'

'You will explain you were in the inn?'

'No! We must . . . ' She took her basket off him and realised that he was teasing her.

'Lie?' He looked into her eyes and she flushed deeply. 'No, miss, you go on your way. I shall be fine now. I will retrieve my horse and make a report. Stay away from this village for a few

15

days. This incident will not go without punishment. Thank you and please do not mention me to anyone — especially to your friend Amie. As far as you are aware I never existed here. Those men would have murdered me, miss. Please do not feel misguided loyalty to them for they would not hold any for you — you helped me escape. I, Russell Deadman, am beholden to you.'

'But I . . . '

He bowed before her, then turned and ran. In moments there was no trace of him ever being there.

Molly looked to the sky; she was late. She was dishevelled and she was, as usual, in trouble, but the memory of a stranger, her friend, bowing to her made her smile.

3

Molly had just laid the plate of cheese, bread and cold meat on the table next to a jug of porter when the cottage door opened and Solomon Platt walked in. She had only had time to brush her hair and pin it up neatly again, then dust the dry mud off her skirt. Although more respectable than she had been by the time she had run back to the cottage, she was far from feeling composed.

He stared at the table, then peered at the newly lit fire and fingered the empty pot still by the side of the open fire instead of hanging over the flames.

'Hello, Father, let me take your coat,' Molly said brightly and started to remove his coat. She was being careful how she slid it over his injured right arm. Although the wound was healed he had limited use in it, which for a rifleman was a harsh fact to accept. He turned around, standing unusually still, and looked at the table.

'Where have you been and what have you been doing? Remember, Molly, lying is a sin.' Slowly he turned his head to face her.

'I'm sorry, Father. The sun was so warm and the trees were so pretty that I forgot that time was going by and . . . I lost track of time.' She looked down.

'Men fight a war against Napoleon, women toil in fields or spend their lives gutting fish to feed their hungry broods, and you watch trees! You can't even cook your father a meal! By hell, girl, the sooner your mother returns with news of a match for you the better. When will you quit this idle dreaming and do your share of work. You eat the food here that I struggle to put on your plate. Do something worthwhile to earn it. I am going to the inn and you, my girl, had better do some work before I return. For if this home is not worthy and ready for your mother's return come tomorrow, I will take my cane to you. Let's see if you can toil now, or are you too stupid that you would rather stare at trees and take a beating for their beauty?'

He grabbed his coat and made for the door.

'I'm sorry, Father. I will do better . . . I'll try. Please stay.'

'Molly, to survive in this world you have to work, not dream. Don't make me thrash you. I'll be back later. I need to let my anger out, for it grieves me, girl, to let loose on you even when you bloody deserve it. Get to work. The sooner you have a husband the better.' He slammed the door behind him.

Molly dearly wanted to tell him the truth about the stranger. Warn him about how ruthless Jeffries and Amos could be. But how could she? How would she begin to explain that she knew who they were, what they did and that she had been in the building watching their brutality? He was going to the inn, but she was never to have set foot near it. Was he a hypocrite or just being a man? Molly set to and scrubbed the cottage clean. She put food in the pot and let a stew cook slowly. It would be there when needed. She would not willingly succumb to the cane, neither did she want to lie to him, but one thing was certain — she did not want to own up to the truth.

Her thoughts turned to her mother and the news she would bring upon her return. She kept picturing the stranger. He had said he would be her friend when he thought her a tavern girl. What sort of man was he? He had a strong face with dark features. His eyes were bright. She thought he looked like a man who had seen the world; or travelled. There was something different about him. Did he really work for the revenue service? If so, he would be a target for every village that plied their trade beyond the guise of fishing. Molly realised that she would never see him again. It was a thought which made her feel slightly saddened because he was far more interesting than any of the local men who talked about the same things day after day. She played with the idea of him being her friend and liked the notion, wondering where he would have taken her if she had kept hold of his hand. It was rough and had been used to work, that she knew, yet his manner and speech showed he was not local but more educated than most she had met.

She forgot all about his other words of advice, telling her to stay away from the inn. Her mind, instead, drifted from her injured friend to her future beau. Who would her mother and aunt feel was suitable for her? They had not looked amongst the local men, but had decided to go to the town of Gorebeck where her aunt now lived, married to a chandler. He owned his own business and was said do be doing well. The town was a place of growing importance. New houses were being built around the old market square. It had a barracks, church and an asylum. Molly had been there once as a child and still remembered the church and the river. Her mother had told her that new shops offered services to the rising number of houses. It was said to be a place with a future as roads crossed here for York, Newcastle, Whitby on the coast, and a road which led west across country. Her mother had been told that young marriageable girls were needed there. She wondered if this meant her future would be married to a soldier like her own mother. Molly hated the thought. She would not accept anyone she did not like, even if it meant rows.

Marriage and life in a town like Gorebeck seemed a world away from their cottage, the old village and the simple town that all combined to make up her home — her world. Would she move there or would the stranger come to this place with its wild weather and superstitious locals?

By the time she had finished working, and wondering, she was so tired that she fell onto her cot and slept soundly.

Solomon was a troubled man. He burst into the inn and saw Amos and Jeffries sitting in the corner looking annoyed. Amos definitely appeared to be agitated.

'What's up, Amos?' he asked. 'You look like you've seen a ghost.'

Solomon closed the door behind him and entered the small dark room.

'Sol, the Revenue's been sniffing around here.' Jeffries was scratching his greasy hair and staring at the flames of the open fire.

'Did you send them on their way?' Solomon sat down on one of the upturned barrels which were used as both seats and tables in this inn on the edge of the beach. The shutters were drawn and the lamps lit within. The shadows flickered around the stone walls. Amos took up most of the space on the settle. Old Amie placed a jug and tankard on the serving hatch then turned into the back room where the store of liquor was kept. Amos moved his ample girth and passed them over to Solomon.

'Him, there was just the one. We roughed him up a bit and took him to the old mill to sweat it out. When we went back he'd gone.' Amos sat back down but shifted uneasily.

'I don't like it. There was something about him which smacked of trouble. We've sent his horse with Jeb over to Ezekiel, so he can't go far away, not quick like,' Jeffries said, before gulping down the last of his porter.

'How did he get free?' Amos asked, scratching his head.

'Not without help he didn't, but then if he had friends around here what do we do? I've told the lads to keep a look out for trouble. There was something about the man, something bothersome. I don't think he'll let it lie.' Jeffries looked at Solomon. 'We should have taken him to the boat. Then we could have lost him, easy like.'

'Why are you here at this hour?' Amos asked Solomon.

'You would have murdered him?' Solomon asked.

Amos looked up, edgy. It was Jeffries who answered.

'He would have joined the navy. No one would have believed him. By the time he was awake he would have been shipped halfway across the seas. He wouldn't have bothered us again. We don't murder folk, do we Amos?'

'No!' the man was adamant — almost too firm. 'So, why're you here?'

'I need warm food in me belly — and that lass of mine, useless she is, offers me nought but cheese and bread. Amie . . . ' he shouted through to the back, 'have you any warm victuals a starving soldier might want?'

'She hasn't, but I have, Solomon Platt.' The voice was warm and friendly, younger than Amie's by many a year.

Solomon smiled. 'Elsie, I was hoping you might be in here. I need . . . ' he glanced at the two men, ' . . . some understanding.'

Amos and Jeffries grinned as they

exchanged knowing looks.

Solomon stood up. 'Excuse me gents, but pleasure before business, eh?' he laughed and placed his good arm around the waist of the young woman who led him out into the night air.

Elsie wasn't much older than his eldest daughter, Muriel, but where she was as thin as a lath, like her mother, Elsie was curvaceous, buxom even. Having lost a man to the French and a son to His Majesty's navy she was a woman alone. Tonight, though, she would have company, or so Solomon thought. He had spent many an hour with her. Molly had got his dander up.

She led him behind the inn, cutting through to her small cottage. He grabbed her arm with his good one and swung her against the inn's wall and started to kiss and fondle her neck and breasts. 'Elsie, I was so hungry till I set eyes upon you.'

She laughed, but tried to push him off her. 'Not here, I have a home, you know. Damn sight less draughty than here too. I don't want old Amie watching us.'

'Sh, woman! She can if she wants. At her age what has she left. We'll hit your cot in a minute. Now you know what Solomon likes.'

If his face had not been buried in her flesh he would have seen the look of disgust in her tired eyes. 'Aye, I do only too well, but tonight you'll not have it,' she whispered.

'Oh, I will. Elsie, once you've let a man have your pleasure you can't turn him away. That's not right. Anyhow, why's that? You feeling awkward?' he mumbled, almost inaudibly.

'Because,' said the stranger's voice, 'tonight Elsie has a new life and you, man, will go to the lock up to start yours.'

Solomon dropped the wench's skirts which he'd started to lift with his good hand, and turned to swing a punch, only to feel the full force of the stranger's fist land upon his jaw. In moments, a group of militia men had swept into the inn. One took Elsie aside. 'You did well, lass.'

She smiled, then ran to her cottage.

When Amos and Jeffries were dragged out and made to kneel before the stranger, it was their turn to feel the blow of an angry fist.

The soldiers had worn dark jackets instead of the uniform red ones in order to approach the inn unseen. Now they worked hard, and by the time the morning light arrived, the inn had been emptied of its liquor — evidence, the soldiers had said as they had loaded it into a boat to be taken down to the bay town further south along the coast.

★ ★ ★

Old Amie had been left with her own things and what food was in her kitchen. The inn was closed. The men and the liquor disappeared and no one knew where they had been taken, except for what the soldier had said about the bay town. Elsie left that night with one of the soldiers. Her cottage was also left bare. The busy old village now looked as though a phantom had struck in the night. Half empty, with souls taken; a silence fell upon it.

★　★　★

Molly awoke on her cot to a very quiet cottage. She heard no snoring or deep breathing from her father's bed. His coat was not upon his peg on the wall. She looked at the stew which was untouched, as was the cheese. She knew she had displeased him and that he had left in a foul temper, but her mother would be back today and there was no sign of her father. She dressed, ate a little something and fixed her bonnet. He'd said he was going to the inn. Whether he approved or not she would have to go there and if he was still laying in a drunken stupor, somehow she would have to drag him up the gill before her mother found out. Her mother did not approve of drinking to excess. In fact she did not believe in anything to excess — laughter, music, food or drink. Their home was sparse and their food simple. After seeing what Amos and Jeffries were capable of, taking another walk to the inn was a journey she did not wish to make.

Her mood changed once she reached the end of the gill when she heard sobbing from behind the inn. To her surprise it was coming from old Amie as she sat upon the back step of the building. A few fisherwomen were standing around her cussing and giving vent to their disgusted feelings as to what had happened the previous night.

Molly approached her timidly.

'Amie . . . ' she began, but as the women spun around and looked at her she stopped.

Amie's red eyes focussed upon her. 'Oh, lass, tis a right mess.'

'What is, Amie? What has happened here?'

'Your pa, Amos, Jeffries and that Jezebel, Elsie Banman, has all gone,'

one of the women said angrily.

'What do you mean, gone? Why would my father go anywhere with Amos and Jeffries?' Molly gripped her knitted shawl tightly to her. The place felt strange and as they stared at her she had never felt quite so alone. 'Who is this Elsie Banman woman?'

'Your father's strumpet,' a woman spat out at Molly, her words bitter and meant to hurt.

Molly took a step back, shocked.

'Don't take it out on the lass, Nell.' Amie stood up. 'Come inside, lass. I'll tell thee what happened.' Amie placed an arm around Molly and led her inside. She sniffed as she crossed the threshold. Molly thought she was about to fold double again in her apparent state of grief, but she seemed to make an effort to straighten up and took a deep breath. 'You best sit down, lass; you're going to be told some things that will shatter your girl-like dreams. I'll start by explaining about Elsie Banman, men, your pa in particular, and how some fools mess with the Revenue and live to regret it.'

Molly swallowed and sat down. She did not know what she was going to hear but she had to prepare to leave childhood behind and face the reality of a world she did not like.

4

Molly stared blankly at the woman whilst trying to stifle the sickening feeling in her stomach. Her father had been taken away from the family. Her own father visited a woman — a harlot, in the village. How was she to explain this to her mother?

'Are you sure about this woman? Are you sure he had a . . . here? Perhaps he was her friend. Don't forget Father was a soldier. He may have been helping a friend's widow. It is possible; in a gesture of charity and compassion he may have helped her. Gossips talk, they make up what they don't know.' Molly looked hopefully at the old lady who almost choked laughing at her, but the good humour did not last.

'Eee, lass. How naïve can thee be? For goodness sake, people see with their own eyes. He hardly hid his 'compassion' from the villagers. He wasn't being charitable; he was making use of a woman who had no man and no money. Heaven forbid you ever end up like Elsie.' She shook her head.

'I would never do such things!' Molly snapped. 'Where have they taken my father?' she asked impatiently.

'God knows. Listen, young miss. Until you've been left with no food, no home and little clothes to wear, you never know what you'd stoop to for a crust to eat. If you've lost your man and child, what is there left to take pride in? So don't go preaching to me and declaring your virtues, unless all you own is the rags on your back. Women fall low when men leave them or are taken away. Lass, men take pleasure from a woman's pain. That's the way of it. Tell your mother to talk to her friends in the big town. My men have gone too, but no one will listen to an old hag. They might listen to a prissy stick. You don't need to mention Elsie to her; there are enough hearts broken already.'

Molly stared at her. Her stomach felt peculiar and her heart heavy. No, it felt as though it was breaking. Even if her father walked into the inn now he would be lost forever. He always instilled the rules of right and wrong in her and her sister. Muriel had been married a year since to a soldier, a lieutenant in the militia at Gorebeck. She had not seen her lovely happy face since they went to the wedding feast. What would she think if she knew about Father? Perhaps her husband, Philip, could help to find him. She cringed at the thought of her father; he was . . . was . . . with a whore from the village. She stood up shakily, nodded at Amie, and left. The village women glared at her. She put her head up and walked past them, mustering what pride she could. As soon as she got to the cover of the wooded gill she ran, ignoring the tears that fell, not stopping until she reached her cottage to wait for her mother.

Her mother's pleasure in returning home to her cottage to bring the good news to her daughter was short lived when the news filtered through. Thinking quickly, and before Philip could return with the small wagon he had used to bring his mother-in-law back home, Molly had been ordered to pack a few things and lock up the cottage. They would return to Gorebeck and from there find out what had befallen her father.

Molly was very quiet on the journey. Her mother stared at her for quite a while. 'You've been crying, child.'

Molly nodded but did not say anything else; instead she looked away. Once they arrived back at Muriel's home, a newly rented town house, her mother's anger was clear, accentuated by her fatigue. The interior was sparse, but presentable, for what her mother hoped would become a family home when her son-in-law was promoted and rose through the ranks. Both Muriel and her mother had ambitions.

Molly jumped down from the wagon and was instantly rewarded by a disapproving look from both Philip and her mother.

'Remember where you are, Millicent!'

Molly opened her mouth to complain, but saw the look of defiance on the older woman's face. She was to use her formal name and not her family's pet name for her whilst in their home.

Muriel greeted them at the door. 'Mother, what is it? Why have you returned so soon?'

'Come, child, we must wait inside whilst Philip makes enquiries at the barracks.'

'Enquiries?' Muriel repeated with a look of panic upon her face.

Her mother stepped over the doorstep of the house and brushed past Molly. She followed on, not looking forward to the inquisition to come. Once the lieutenant had left them alone her mother stood before her. 'Now,

Molly my girl, tell me the truth of it.'

'Father went out last night. There was a raid at the inn and it was said that he was somehow taken up in it. No one knows where he is. No one has been told anything.'

'Why was he in the village last night?' Her mother glared at her.

'He wanted to go to the inn. I suppose he wanted to drink. He didn't say, why.' Molly looked from one to the other, giving the truth where she could and hiding the facts she didn't want them to know as long as possible. If she had cooked his dinner he would not have gone to the inn in the first place. The stranger might be dead or injured, but her father would be safe. Then there was the woman, Elsie. Perhaps he would have wanted to go anyhow. But she couldn't tell her mother that. How could she?

'Why?' her mother asked.

'Why what, Mother?' Molly repeated.

'He didn't want us to associate with the villagers, so why would he go there?' She was staring at her. Her mother could tell when she was hiding something. She always had been able to.

'To drink, Mother, I suppose.' Molly looked away. Muriel caught her eye. Her vexed eyes served only to annoy Molly further.

'How do you know what happened?' Muriel asked.

'I went down this morning and spoke to an old woman who lives at the inn. She told me what happened and asked if I could ask you to find out where their menfolk were and why.' Molly was defiant.

'You went to an inn!' Muriel snapped.

'How else was I to find out what happened?' she protested, but both the other women were looking upon her with visible disgust.

'If Lieutenant Deadman hears of this, your future will be ruined, girl.' Her mother was incensed.

'Lieutenant Deadman? You know

him.' Molly's surprise at the mention of the name seemed to wrong foot the other women.

'More to the point, how would you know Lieutenant Deadman?' her mother asked.

'I don't. Not really . . . not at all. I have heard the name somewhere.' Molly fidgeted. 'What is he to Father?'

'Nothing, as yet. He will be his son-in-law if we can find Solomon before word of this 'misunderstanding' gets out, or that his intended has been seen in an inn!' Her mother glared at her. 'I came home to tell you the good news that James has shown a serious interest in you. Although what type of a wife you will make I dread to think. Where is Philip? Why does he take so long?' The older lady seated herself by the fire and sighed heavily.

'Who is James?' Molly asked.

'Lieutenant James Deadman. Do you know him or not?' Muriel asked.

'No . . . Not at all.' Molly's heart was beating ever faster. The loss of her father was hard enough to come to terms with on its own without a new confusion to deal with. 'Once we know Father is safe I will consider this man, but first let's find Father.'

'Millicent, you will do more than consider this man. He is quite taken by you. He has seen you at church and watched you from afar. James would very much like you to be his wife, despite the disapproval of his family. They have even sent his cousin here to dissuade him from marrying beneath his class. James is from a family who have had position, and land, but who have hit financially difficult times. They are shunned by their own kind for having to move away from the city and buy up a small manor house here amongst what they consider uncivilised country folk. It is said that his cousin has even entered into trade in order to keep the family together, and he educated in Edinburgh. It is all too much for them, but Lieutenant James Deadman wants a wife who is used to work and has no ideas of grandeur. You, he thinks, fits his ideal.'

'Have you met his cousin?' Molly asked.

Muriel laughed. 'I have, and I must say a more self impressed man I have not met. He holds himself in high esteem. I should not think he will deter poor James, though, for he talks to everyone with contempt and derision.' Muriel held her head high.

'What is his name?'

'Dr Russell Deadman,' she answered. 'I believe he has been snooping around Ebton trying to find out all he can about our family, especially Father. James told me he seems to fancy himself as one of Lord Wellington's intelligence officers.' She scoffed, 'I ask you. How low can one stoop? Father is worth a hundred such wastrels. I hope the townsfolk sent him off with a flea in his ear.'

Molly paled. She stared at the flames. So that was why the man was asking questions. He was searching for information on her father. Had he found out about Elsie? He must have. She had rescued a man who did not think her worthy of a marriage to his own cousin. She swallowed and closed her eyes. What a mess this was. Her family would be the talk of the district and poor Muriel had tried so hard to improve her lot, making Father out to be a war hero, and her mother the virtuous woman of the town. What had she done?

'Are you all right, girl?' her mother asked.

'I don't know. What if our father has been sent away? Pressed or something. What do we do then?'

'We cope like I have coped the many years when he was away overseas.' There was an icy tone to her mother's voice. 'Until Philip returns we should not think the worst. Is there something else you wish to tell me, Molly?'

Molly looked straight at her mother and answered honestly, 'There is nothing else I wish to tell you, Mother, of that I'm certain.'

She, too, sat down and continued to stare at the flames wondering if the stories of hell were true and if she was destined to be sent there because she could not say the truth of it, yet to withhold the truth was, in a way, lying. Either way, she felt doomed.

5

An hour passed by before Philip returned to the house. Molly could see that the usually calm lieutenant was greatly flummoxed; his high colour and agitated manner accentuated the effect of his current mood. He ran a nervous finger around the inside of his collar which now appeared to be too tight for him in his state of unease.

'What news do you bring us, sir?' Muriel stood up as he entered the parlour and rushed over to him.

Molly thought his manner appeared to be strange. He could hardly bring himself to look at any of them, especially Muriel. He was normally confident, attentive and a good host.

'Dr Deadman will arrive shortly. He has some unpleasant news and wishes to speak to you, ma'am, in private.' He looked at his mother-in-law.

'Why would he wish to speak with me now, at such a time? Can it not wait, sir? Surely it is more important that we have word of my dear husband first?' Her eyes seemed almost watery. She was not a woman given to fits of emotion but Molly was sure that those pale grey eyes looked sad and tired.

'No!' Molly also stood. She was adamant that if the man had anything to say to her mother, then he could say it in front of her too. The truth might have to come out, but she wanted to be there to protect her mother and defend herself if necessary.

'Millicent, it would be better if you left the room; you too, Muriel. This will be a difficult enough conversation without young ladies being present. He glanced at Molly as he said the word 'ladies' as if he was gracing her with a questionable title.

Molly stood by her mother and placed a hand on the older woman's shoulder. 'I'm not leaving, Mother. I won't leave you to face this man alone.'

Her mother's curious eyes looked up at her. They were questioning her silently as if she knew her daughter well enough to realise that something was definitely amiss with her. 'Perhaps it would be best if we all stayed together. This man cannot have anything so shocking to say about your father that my girls should not be aware of. Unless, that is, he is injured.' A look of panic crossed her face.

'No, he is in fine health. Just a little discomforted.'

'Well there is nothing this man can tell me about Solomon that I do not already know. I am quite sure.' She sniffed.

Molly stared at the top of her mother's bonnet and wondered how she could remain in ignorance of the true nature of the man she had married for so long.

'He is not injured in any way, ma'am,' Philip replied quickly and gave an anxious Muriel a reassuring nod. 'However, there are issues that Dr

Deadman wishes to discuss that may be indelicate.'

'Then the family will stay together, Philip, and this creature will address us with whatever news he has. I know he is a ferret of a man, a weasel who would lurk in the dark and try to besmirch the good name of an innocent man and taint his family. I am ready to face him.'

Molly squeezed her shoulder gently but she saw the strange look in Philip's eyes. He was deeply concerned about something. Molly was about to demand he brought the charade to a close by telling them what the matter was that was so disturbing but realised it could be very embarrassing to them all if he blurted out about the woman, Elsie. They heard the door being answered by their maid. Her little figure announced at the door of the parlour the arrival of Dr Deadman.

Molly felt her mother straighten her back. Molly herself removed her hand and stepped back behind the sofa and stared as the familiar figure stepped confidently into the room. He carried a bruise to his cheek and she remembered how pitiful and frightened he had been as he gratefully thanked her for rescuing him. Now she wondered if she had done the correct thing. Was he about to destroy her family?

His eyes looked to her mother first. He then removed his top hat and nodded to Muriel before addressing the seated lady. It was as if he had failed to take in Molly's presence at first. She stood stock still.

'Mrs Platt, I presume,' he said, with little grace.

'You presume correctly, sir.' She met his gaze.

'I would prefer to speak to you in private.' He turned to Philip who looked away, glancing imploringly at Muriel.

'My daughters wish to stay with me and I see no reason why they should not as our discussion must surely concern the whereabouts of my poor husband.'

'Daughters?' He saw Molly, as if realising for the first time she was not an invisible servant.

'You . . . ' he began to speak out, but was interrupted by her mother.

'This is Millicent, my youngest daughter, and Muriel who is the lady of the house. Now please tell me where my husband is and what has happened to him before I become ill with the worry of it all.'

He was still staring at Molly. 'You are the sister to be matched to my cousin, James . . . you?'

'I do not know about that issue, but I want to know where my father is, and why you are here?' Molly tried to bring him back to the matter to be discussed and hopefully away from their previous meeting.

'Sir, I am well aware that you so heartily disapprove of the match, so let us cut to the chase . . . Where is my husband?'

He returned his attention to Mrs Platt. 'He is shortly to be released from the gaol with a warning. He was in the presence of . . . ' He hesitated, and Molly interrupted.

'Sir, if he is to be released, why has he been warned and why are you here?' Molly asked, praying he would not mention the woman, Elsie.

'He was in the presence of smugglers, drinking illicit brandy and behaving . . . badly.' He sighed and looked at Molly. 'I have arranged his release. Lieutenant Trenton does not need his good family name linked to a man who frequents taverns and mixes with felons. He has been released to try to wash the stain from this good family. Madam, I will not take the issue further, but I would strongly request you relinquish this half-baked notion that you have to match your daughter to my cousin . . . For both of their sakes.'

'How dare you speak to my mother in such a way? You are a bully and a brute!' Muriel shouted at him.

'Muriel, behave like a lady!' Lieutenant Trenton snapped, causing Muriel to burst into tears and flee the room.

'Satisfied, sir?' Mrs Platt commented.

'No, not yet! Will you drop this match?' he persisted.

Lieutenant Trenton was obviously shaken by both Muriel's and his outburst. 'Excuse me, sir,' he left the room in search of his wife.

'Why are you so against my family?' Molly asked.

He thought for a moment choosing his words with care. 'I cannot say all, but, miss, I would say this. He is not the man for you.'

'Who would be then?' Molly's mother asked brazenly. 'You?'

The question took him by surprise or, Molly wondered, if it was disgust which caused his cheeks to flush as he replaced the hat upon his head.

'Mrs Platt, your husband shamed himself last night. I will see that he is freed and that the shame goes no further, but you must promise that this marriage match is severed and all notion of it scuppered.'

'And, sir, if it is not?' Mrs Platt asked.

'I fear that the gossip would affect your daughter Muriel deeply and Lieutenant Trenton's prospects adversely also. Good day, ma'am.' He bowed slightly then turned to Molly. 'Miss.' He left the room.

Molly ran out into the hall after him, ignoring her mother's protestations.

'How dare you. I saved your life and you try to ruin mine. What type of beast are you?' Molly was only a foot from him, almost whispering her words to him. Despite the barely audible voice there was no taking away the tone in which they were said.

'You saved my life and I have just spared your father. I also spared your mother the pain of knowing he was whoring when he was arrested, or that her daughter who would wed into my family, frequented inns. So, Miss Millicent, what type of beast am I? Answer your own question and believe me when I say James is not the man for you. Good day.' He opened the door and stepped out into the town without glancing back.

Molly turned around to see her mother watching her from the doorway. 'What was that about, Molly?' The woman folded her arms.

Molly shrugged. 'He insists his cousin would not make me happy.'

'Did he? Perhaps not, but girl, you could make him a happy man and he has more to offer you than you do him.' She reached out a hand to her daughter who took it in hers. 'Molly, be careful of that man. He is no fool and he is proud, too proud to accept the likes of our family into his. Men like that are dangerous. We will have to take care in our arrangements.'

'But, Mother, you heard him. We must stop the matchmaking or else he will spread gossip that would damage Philip's prospects.' Molly tried to soften her manner as she stood before her mother. She loved the lady dearly, but Muriel had more in common with her.

Molly was not taken by the idea of being a hostess, attending assemblies or venturing to the city. She knew the people would hate her as 'common' so why try to belong where you just don't.

'Will he, though? It could have been an idle threat. We shall have to be clever then, shall we not? Perhaps our good doctor has secrets to hide. I will speak to James about it, but you will carry on your normal life and say nothing to anyone. Dr Deadman is not as clever at handling people as he thinks he is. He may just have met his match.'

Molly flushed slightly, feeling very uneasy as a smile crossed her mother's face. The world had become a strange place. She was still holding the door open when the figure of her father came into view. He looked shaken and angry.

'Leave us,' her mother said, and gestured she should retreat quickly into the house. Molly slipped back inside and left her mother to speak with him alone. The parlour door was closed after he entered, but loud muffled words resounded around the house shortly afterwards. There would be little rest for anyone this evening. Molly hoped that tomorrow the sun would shine again, but as far as her father was concerned, he now had a permanent cloud over him . . . named Elsie.

6

Molly's father was very quiet the following morning. He ate his breakfast in silence. The lieutenant had left early and the mood in the room was tense between husband and wife. Molly looked at Muriel who was dabbing her lip with a napkin. She raised her eyebrows at her sister in a gesture of despair.

'You must stay in town for a few days, Father. I am sure the change will do you both good.' Muriel smiled at him as she placed her napkin neatly by her plate. 'Now that the little misunderstanding has been sorted out you could go with Philip to his club. I am sure we can sort something out for you to wear and . . . '

'I am sure that you mean well, Muriel, but your father will be returning to Ebton today. Molly and I will stay until the end of the week. We have things to see to. Could you possibly let her share some of your dresses, dear? She came ill prepared. However, my trunk is still in the wagon.' Her mother folded her napkin and placed it on her plate. 'Your father needs time to sort out his affairs.'

'Of course, Mother.' Muriel turned to face her father. 'I could have my doctor see you if you wish.'

'No, lass, I don't want a doctor. I'll go back home ... ' He looked at Prudence, his wife of over twenty two years and added, 'It would be for the best. I'll make sure all is well for your return. We'll put this behind us soon enough.' He was still staring at his wife but there was a more determined note in his voice which made it more of a command than a statement.

Prudence nodded, acknowledging the comment, rose and left the room. Muriel followed her out, but Molly hesitated.

'I'm sorry I had not prepared a hot

meal for you, Father. Perhaps if I had you would not have been caught up in the trouble.' She looked at him; his eyes were still bloodshot. He did not smell of alcohol so she presumed it was due to lack of sleep.

He did not speak for a moment. 'I should have given you a beating. Not for the food, but for time wasting, girl.' He leaned over to her. 'Just before they swooped on the poor folk in the inn I had been told of someone who had been interfering where they'd no business. Someone had helped a man escape from trouble he had invited upon himself, by asking too many questions where he had no business knowing the answers. Someone helped him get away. I'm betting that that someone was busy daydreaming where they had no right to be and saw more than they ought to. If he had not been freed no one would be in gaol now. He would be working his way in His Majesty's navy across the seas, instead of messing up your mother's plans for your wedding. Lass, now we have no inn. Old Amie has no one to look after her and you'll be lucky to marry a fisherman . . . '

Without taking her attention from his face, she answered him directly, 'You talk in riddles, Father. If a man was being held in fear of being pressed then surely he needed freeing. You have sworn about the antics and operations of the pressgangs for years. So if 'someone' freed this man then they must have been acting honourably. Old Amie has the villagers to look out for her and she knows how an inn runs. She will not be short of volunteers to help her, I'm sure. Nelly will see her right. Father, you are saying that the people in the village had apprehended a free man and were going to wreck his life. How can that be right?' Molly continued to stare at him.

He was not used to her standing her ground and answering him back in such a worldly way. Solomon looked uncertain for a second, as if he was not sure if she was innocent of the act or guilty as sin. She kept a straight, and she hoped what was a pious face.

'What would you know of Nelly and the villagers?' he asked in a quiet voice.

'Not a lot, but when I went there to ask Old Amie if you were still there in the morning she told me what happened the previous night, when the soldiers came and you were taken away. Apparently there were three men and a woman who were spirited away. I pity the woman. Life is hard enough for a man on his own, but a woman is so vulnerable and must face such hardships.' She toyed with the napkin.

He stood up and slammed his fist down on the table. 'You keep that mouth of yours shut. You speak of what you have no notion. You do as your mother says and we'll find you a husband who will curb your insolence. Do not dare to speak of such things in your mother's presence, girl. You know nothing of this world and its ways beyond looking after a cottage and daydreaming.'

Molly pushed back her chair, staying as calm as she could. By doing so she was no longer in the shadow of his figure anymore as he had leaned over her. She stood up and walked over to the door. 'I will marry a man of my own choosing. No matter what Dr Deadman, Mother or you think. I shall not be farmed off to anyone who meets your criteria without him meeting my own. I have my own, sir. This is my life and it is my body, I shall not trade it to the highest bidder! Good day, Father. I shall see you at the end of the week.' She left the room quickly, collected her sister's muff and coat from the maid, informing her to tell her mother that she needed to take the air, and walked out of the house.

Her father shouted something after her but he did not follow her out. His energy, like his temper, appeared spent. Molly had little reason to stay. By the time they met again they would both have had time to calm down, she hoped.

Molly kept walking until she was standing by the river bank near the bridge. She watched a family of ducks follow their mama down the stream. She wished so much she too could just drift off away from all that had happened, and her father. She felt a tear threaten to run down her cheek and quickly she checked it. What a fool she had been, but even though it had changed her life, she did not regret rescuing the stranger. She did not know if her father really knew it was her or if he was just guessing, but unless Dr Deadman revealed the truth it would remain her secret. If the villagers knew it to be her she would never be able to return home. They held long grudges and whether their menfolk were in the right or the wrong, they had been taken and that was down to her actions.

Molly had created another mess, but beyond this was the stark reality that her straight-laced father who had brought both her and her sister up quite strictly had been with a whore. Not just the once, but had used the woman on a regular basis. No wonder he did not want her wandering down there. Her poor mother, she thought. Molly sniffed, barely able to stop the tears. She had always respected him but now her heart ached for her mother whom he had betrayed. He was no more than a bully and user of women. She felt a hand upon her shoulder, which snapped her out of her thoughts.

'Miss Platt, I think you should walk with me a while.' Dr Deadman was standing next to her. His black coat, cane and hat gave him a look of elegance and sophistication that had been lacking when she had rescued him in the mill. 'Please, let us walk through the churchyard, there is a wooded path beyond where we can talk privately. There we shall be unseen from prying eyes and be free to talk openly with each other.'

'I should return,' she began to say,

but was trying to avoid looking at him through her saddened eyes.

'We must talk, miss, and besides, your father has not left the house yet.' He smiled at her surprise. 'Lieutenant Trenton has kept me informed of events, and I gather that your mother is far from pleased that her husband had been found in an inn. To my knowledge she is not aware of his trollop.' He paused. 'I am sorry to be so blunt, miss. Let us please walk and talk, as friends. I would like us at least to be that.'

'You are very arrogant, sir!' she snapped.

'Yes.' He cupped her elbow and gently walked her through the church's gates.

'This is highly improper.' Molly objected, but did nothing to turn away.

'Yes, but then so are you,' he said simply.

She let out a gasp of indignation.

'Oh, don't act so hurt, miss. You can hardly deny it. You hide in inns and then rescue idiots who have got themselves into a desperate scrape. Neither are the doings of a lady, are they?' Reluctantly she smiled back at him, wiping the last of her tears from the corner of her eye. 'That's much better. You would be no match for James, believe me.'

'Why should I?' He stopped once they were beyond the church and in the cover of the trees.

'He likes to hunt. Do you?'

She shrugged. 'I have never been on one.'

'He likes to entertain. Do you?'

'I have been told I can be very entertaining at times.' She stared at him as he smiled at her words.

'He has an appetite for alcohol. Have you?' he persisted.

'I have not been allowed to partake of it. Father does not believe it is fitting for a lady to drink alcohol.' She watched a bird land on the upper branches of a tree, ignoring the scoffing sound he made.

'He wants a wife before the autumn

because he would take her with him to war ... Someone who will keep him warm and comfortable on a night, when he has such an uncertain future during the daylight hours. Not many young ladies of good families are that keen to send their daughters to war with such a man. So by looking at the lower orders he can take someone who is expendable in an awkward situation. Should you both return healthy, you will spend years producing children whilst he visits his various clubs in town — London that is, not Ebton.'

She turned and stared at him. 'You have a callous tongue, sir. I am expendable, am I?'

'In his eyes ... yes.'

'What do you say, sir? How do you view me and why would your family send you here to stop a match if I was destined to go where no 'lady of repute' would?' She was standing square to him.

'I say that my family heard he planned to marry and I was sent to 'look over' the situation. I have since found out his reasons and his intentions. I did not know you, Miss Millicent, but would have warned any naïve girl who fell for his charms. I had found out some unsavoury facts concerning your father. That led me to believe his offspring would be seeking to better themselves through the link. I presumed your family would have followed his example. However, your mother is more of a lady than he a gentleman. I believe she married beneath her.'

'He thought to better himself perhaps. Many do. It is the way of the marriage mart, is it not? Surely you are not so naïve as to believe in love.' This time it was her turn to scoff at him.

He paused and took a moment to reply. 'I believe that you have not met James. I suggest you do not. If you are forced to, turn the other cheek and walk away. It is better the match talk ceases for everyone's well-being.' His posture had become more rigid, his manner more abrupt and his eyes less friendly.

'Tell me, sir. Do you stop at nothing to get your own way?'

'I do not like to be crossed. You have seen what happens to those who do. I have been lenient on your father. He could easily have been taken to York with Amos and Jeffries. They will stand at the next assizes. There was enough stashed contraband to nail them without mentioning my attempted murder. In keeping this out of the frame I have kept our secret safe and not involved you directly. You are only involved by association, that is, as the daughter of your father.'

He was looking down at her, his manner cold, unlike the friendly way they had started their conversation. Why? Had he been annoyed at her mentioning love?

'What will you do with the woman, Elsie?' Molly asked, feeling awkward at mentioning her name.'

'I shall wish her well. She has agreed

to go with one of the soldiers. He lost his wife in childbirth and she has no man to protect her from lechers. So at least she has a life to live now with a future.' There was a challenge in his voice; he obviously loathed her father.

'You don't know him, sir. My father fought valiantly and came back less of a man because of it.' Molly half-heartedly defended him.

'Did he? Or was he always a bully and a coward who could lord it over women but who didn't measure up in a battle?'

Molly backed away two steps. 'You make judgements as if you were God. How dare you? At least he went to war. Tell me, why have you not? Are you exempted because you are a doctor? Perhaps you would be needed more with the army than here, but they may not pay you so well and your hands may be soiled!'

'You have a sharp wit and an even sharper tongue, woman. You do not know me and I have no reason to explain myself. Take my words seriously and heed my warnings or you will suffer.'

'You threaten me, sir. Yet it is my father you call a bully. I shall meet James Deadman and I will decide what happens next . . . not you, not Father, but me. You crashed into my life. Now walk out of it.' She turned and stormed off.

On the air his words reached her ears, 'You are a fool, Molly.' She ignored them and continued walking until she was safely back in the grounds of the church. Her father was just leaving the town, seated beside Philip on the wagon. Neither saw her but both men were travelling in silence staring ahead of them. Why had she defended him so virulently when Russell Deadman had been so right? He was a bully and a hypocrite and always had been. Perhaps he was even a coward. She returned to the house with her heart heavy once more and her head full of doubts.

★ ★ ★

Dr Russell Deadman stayed by the trees watching the river flow by and seeing a family of ducks floating along; a mother with her brood. He thought about the spirited young woman and groaned inside. James was not right for her. He had wanted to break the match before it was set. That was when he knew that she was the brat of a discharged sergeant who he thought was trying to muscle in on his cousin. Now, having met her and seeing what a caring, naïve girl she was, he was determined to stop it for her own sake. Only he had a lack of talent with words. He was too forthright. He knew what to do with bodies but lacked the ability to trade polite banter where such issues were concerned. Besides all of this, she was to him like an angel sent to him in his darkest time. He had never known fear until those few moments when he was strung up in the darkness of the mill. He had so much he wanted to live for and she had made him realise just how much. He would stop a union between James and Molly if he had to. His problem now was how to do it without having his angel hate him for it.

7

The following morning Molly borrowed one of Muriel's better day dresses, a matching velvet spencer and a bonnet. Together, the sisters walked into the town on an errand for their mother.

Muriel would not be drawn about her father's behaviour or the row between their mother and him. It was, she said, too unpleasant a subject to discuss, and instead chose to lecture and advise Molly on how a lady should keep house for her husband. How she should behave when in the company of her betters and how not to rub people up the wrong way.

Molly was hardly listening to her perpetual drone, so lost was she in thought remembering the previous day's outing with Dr Deadman. How could someone be so rude, arrogant and yet still fill her mind with his presence every waking moment of her day. Molly reasoned that it must be the effect of the upset at home. She was obviously trying to avoid the issue in her own way, like her sister did in refusing to talk about it instead filling her days with tittle-tattle of the most inconsequential kind.

They were standing outside the haberdashers admiring a length of ribbon when a joyful sounding voice disturbed them. 'Mrs Trenton, how delightful it is to see you looking so divine.'

Muriel turned and blushed, fawning just a little as she addressed the rather handsome looking lieutenant who had joined them.

'Lieutenant Deadman, what a surprise and a delight to see you here.' Muriel's eyes almost sparkled as she looked over to her sister.

Molly could always tell when her sister was lying. The soldier was quite a delight to the eye, tall, with mid brown hair cut fashionably short, a strong slim physique and grey-green eyes.

He turned his attention to Molly and smiled broadly. 'Miss Millicent Platt, what a joy to meet you in person at last. I have heard so much about you that I can only say the compliments do not do you sufficient justice.'

Molly blushed, although inside what she really felt was a strong impulse to cringe. His flattery was so generous — too good to be true. Yet she was determined not to show her feelings lest Dr Deadman was spying on them as they stood there in the street.

'You really are too kind, sir.' Molly managed to smile, but her eyes were scanning the doorways of the buildings opposite looking for a dark figure, lurking in the shadows, wearing his black coat which suited his dour countenance so well.

'May I walk with you?' he asked sweetly.

'I must pop in here, lieutenant, but please, Millicent, take the air with the good lieutenant. I shall join you shortly.' Muriel nodded at Molly who gave her a hint of a displeased look, but was too polite to be outright rude to this stranger who had designs upon her future. She tried to overlay all the cruel things that his cousin, Russell, had said about him, but she found it difficult because he had such a happy manner about him.

They walked a few moments in silence.

'May I call you Miss Millicent?' he asked timidly.

'Yes, you may,' she answered. 'Do I call you lieutenant all the time, sir?'

'I hardly think that will be necessary unless we are in company. Let us say that between just the two of us we shall be Millicent and James. How is that?'

She looked at him and could not help herself smile. He had a way with him that made her feel at ease.

'That would be fine, James,' she reasoned.

'You have heard that I am interested in you, Millicent, and that I would very much like you to consider me as a possible suitor? I am sorry to be so direct; however, time is not on my side. I may be recalled to London in the next few weeks and therefore I need to be quite bold in my intentions.' He slowed the pace down as they reached the end of the main street. 'Please, let us continue a little way up the lane. There is a quiet place by the river where we may talk and perhaps learn to understand each other. I have been invited to dine with your sister's family and your mother, but I really think we need a few moments alone. Do you agree?'

Molly hesitated for a moment and then decided that he was right. They should make the most of the few moments together. It may be the only chance she would have to actually find out what the man had in his mind and in his character.

'Very well, but only a short while. I do not wish to be seen as a young lady who disappears with young gentlemen at will. It would distress my mother greatly if she found out.' Molly saw a look of concern cross his face.

'I shall be very discreet, Millicent. This way,' he said, and led her down a short track which took them to the river bank. He then held her hand and led her under the cover of a weeping willow tree to a place on the bank at the other side of it where there was only the one way in and the one way out. She had to stop to gather her skirts so that they did not catch on the undergrowth.

'However did you find this place?' she asked. It was just like one of her special places in the gill; so near to folk and yet so private. If it was known she was there with a man, unchaperoned, her reputation, such as it was, would be in ruins, yet she loved the feeling of freedom and felt a familiar rush of daring as she looked around her. The family of ducks swam past and she beamed at them, loving the closeness. She could have reached out and touched one of the babies if she had wished to, but she would not dream of frightening them as they went happily on their way. When she turned around she saw the lieutenant was watching her closely.

'You are quite exquisite, Millicent. You see beauty in the most common place of things. Most girls would not look twice at them.' He moved near to her.

'I do not know 'most girls', but if they cannot see the beauty in such creatures then they are missing out on a lot in life. Nature is one of the few things which is free and is all around us.' She waved her arms in the air as if to encompass the whole of creation.

'I can see only one thing of beauty, Millicent. A person who is so natural and has no knowledge of how exquisite she really is,' he almost whispered to her, his voice was so soft. With one finger he flicked a wayward strand of her hair from her face. It was such a simple gesture yet even his fleeting touch stirred something within her. It was as if he had somehow made a very personal gesture.

She turned away, unsure how to react to him or what to say to him in reply. The ducks had gone. They were alone, her and a strange man.

He placed his hands gently on her shoulders as she looked away. Then he pointed to a wild cat that had caught a field mouse on the opposite bank. 'Look!' he said excitedly.

His mouth was next to her ear, his breath warm against her skin.

Molly was lost in a moment of mixed thoughts. She stared at the cat playing with the hapless mouse and wondered if that was what he was doing with her. He was confident and handsome; she would have loved to have turned around and seen what his embrace felt like, to discover what his intentions were, but the words of Dr Russell Deadman rang in her ears, cutting across the moment.

He rested his chin gently on her shoulder, turning his head slowly so that his lips chanced a kiss on her neck.

It was too much. She moved away from him. 'I think I should return. Muriel will worry if she cannot find me.'

'You have no concerns there, Millicent. It was she who arranged for our little meeting with your mother's blessing. I know Russell has no doubt said damning things about me. It is his way. He is bound by propriety and . . . well . . . not to put too fine a point on it he is jealous.' James shrugged and picked up a blade of grass from the ground, playing with it between his fingers.

'Why is he jealous of you, James?' she asked, her curiosity obvious.

He smiled at her and looked a little awkward as he seemed to search for the words to answer her with. 'Because I was favoured by both my father and his brother, Russell's father. You see he has always been serious, bookish, he cannot relax into nature as I can, and indeed as I see you can. He was happier studying whilst I was out riding, fencing, wrestling, dancing . . . living life as I thought it should be. I am a soldier, Millicent, my future is more uncertain than those who are not.' He moved closer to her again. 'There was a girl he wanted to marry who unfortunately preferred me. He never forgave me for taking her attention away from him. How was I to know what was in the girl's mind? I was only being polite as she was commonly plain, not at all the type of young lady who would take my eye. He blamed me because she realised she could not be happy with him. Now he seeks to destroy my peace again.' He looked down and sighed. Then he focussed on her eyes appealingly. 'Shall we let him, Millicent? Or shall we say it is our life and dare to live it?' He took hold of both her hands and lifted them to his lips, kissing them quickly, grinning impishly. 'I can take you such places, show you such wonders and share my love with you for I am a creature who likes to be open, unlike poor Russell who must always hide from his own desires. He wants to be looked up to. I only seek to be loved and I shall love in return, tenfold. Millicent, I lost my heart to you at your sister's wedding. My foolishness was not to step forward and tell you about my feelings sooner. Forget Russell and his idle threats, he is no more than a coward hiding behind his doctor's bag to avoid fighting for his country like a man.' He shook his head. 'I apologise, I go too far. Forgive me you did not need to know that. Just ignore his words for he is a bitter man.'

Molly was swept away in the rush of his confessions. She had never had anyone, let alone a handsome soldier, talk to her in such a straightforward and direct way before. She could not think what to say. Her hesitation gave him his moment to act. He stepped forward, swept her up in an embrace and kissed her with a fiery passion on her lips. Her senses were confused, her defences down, her mind completely baffled and her body filled with such emotions and feelings that she knew not what to do.

He had revealed his heart to her and confided his deepest concerns and feelings for her and those he had carried in that heart about his cousin. The two men were as different as chalk and cheese. One straight-laced and the other daring and fun. The mother duck quacked as her brood returned.

Millicent was snapped back into the reality of what was happening. With a huge effort she pushed him away and wiped her mouth delicately on the back of her glove. She was almost shaking, but he stepped away from her and with that same impish grin looked on her sheepishly. She remembered a different face, the scared eyes of Russell when she found him in the mill and wondered if it was more than a natural fear. Was the man a coward?

'I wanted you to know, Millicent, what my love is like. I know we have just met, but time and place waits for no one. Forgive me. I hope I did not disappoint you.' He pointed to her bonnet that had slipped a little.

Molly quickly readjusted her dress and breathed in deeply. 'It is time I returned. Don't ever try that again. I am not 'that' sort of girl; despite my more humble beginnings I am from a respectable family, James.'

'No, I know you are not, but you could easily be 'that' kind of wife, the type who dares to enjoy her body and the way a man can make it feel. We shall now return.'

Molly followed him along the track which would lead them back to the town. 'I will not. I cannot be your wife, James.' Molly plucked up courage to declare.

Immediately he stopped and faced her. 'I am not a monster, Millicent. I thought I had explained that I am acting out of character because I have not the time to court you as I would wish to — as you deserve to be. Please don't run scared of me, for I would never knowingly harm or frighten you.'

His sincerity touched her. 'If I marry you, Dr Russell Deadman will ruin my sister's life. The situation is impossible.'

A cloud seemed to blot out James' sunny disposition. 'I will not let him. If he threatens to besmirch the character of those lovely people I shall destroy his.' He attempted to smile.

'You have the knowledge of his past? Is there a skeleton within the good doctor's closet?'

She watched as a slow smile spread across his face and the sparkle appeared in his eyes. 'Oh yes, my dear, no one is perfect. Leave my cousin to me and rejoice that your future is about to be filled with joy.'

He winked at her and she could not help but smile at him. Was he really so happy and playful? He reminded her of a puppy they had once had which never let anything get in its way to stop it getting what it wanted. Strange that she should think that, because hadn't she accused Russell of being determined to get his own way no matter what the cost? James, though, had a playful side to him that Russell lacked.

He moved the tree branches from her way and in silence she returned to the high street, where her sister was just walking down the road towards her, smiling.

8

Molly was very quiet when they met up with Muriel again.

James kissed her hand and took his leave of them. She watched him walk down the road; he was a striking and an athletic figure who looked very fine in his uniform.

'He seems very pleased, Molly. You have obviously impressed him greatly. Is it set then. Are you accepting his offer?' Muriel tried hard to find out what had happened between her and James.

'I have not said I will or I won't,' she said dismissively. Molly would not say anything one way or another.

Once home, they entered the parlour where their mother was seated by the window as if busily employed working her embroidery. She had obviously been watching along the street.

'Ah, my girls return.' She smiled

warmly at them and placed her handiwork down on a small highly polished marquetry table.

Both sat down. Molly stared across the room. She wanted to go and rest. Molly had much to think over. She needed to ponder over the myriad of conflicting information she had heard about both men. James was such an interesting and fun person to be with. So how could Russell say he was not right for her? Hadn't she shown herself to be far from prissy? If what James said was true, Russell was a very bitter man and a coward. Why would a coward venture into such a place as the inn on his own. He had hardly crumpled before Amos and Jeffries when they hit him. If anything, he had looked defiant. It was so confusing. She would prefer time to sort her feelings out before having to decide who was telling her the truth — or was that just it. They both were but were also seeing things very differently. If her mother and sister were not so keen to see her wed to this man, James, she would have no doubt accepted his offer then and there. The thought of facing her father again after being so outspoken and him knowing that his secret was known to her, made her feel like eloping with James that day. Hasty, she thought. He offered her excitement, fun and challenge. Her life would never be dull and that kiss had made her feel quite different inside. Exciting was the word she could find to best fit her emotions. Then there was Dr Russell Deadman to consider. He would stop the match anyway. Why? For jealousy, perhaps. Was he a coward and a man given to snobbery and vengeance? This together made another reason why she should accept James out of hand. But were any of these reasons justifiable? Her head spun with more questions than answers. She needed time and space — her own. Neither did she have.

'You must excuse me, Mother. I wish to rest. I have much to consider.' Molly stood up and took two quick steps towards the door.

'No, I must not and will not excuse you, my girl. You will sit yourself down and tell me all. Time is precious and I am not wasting a second of it. What happened between the two of you along that path?' Her mother took her hand and led her to the window seat so that she could sit next to her. 'I saw him whisk you away.'

'James has declared he would like me to be his wife and needs to know my answer within a very short time.' Molly glanced out of the window as a rider passed by. Tall, handsome, wearing full riding outfit and what looked like the army boots of a cavalry man. She was surprised to see it was Dr Deadman. He looked younger when not wearing the formal black attire. Molly looked back at her mother as she was aware that her voice had gained momentum and become higher.

'You did say yes, didn't you? He is the most appealing of men. Surely you would not be so foolish as to turn him down? You can tell me all, girl. I want to know the truth. Has he propositioned you in any way? If you miss this man there are many in York and Harrogate, with better prospects, who will snap him up.'

'No, Mother, I did not refuse him. Neither did I accept him. I need to think his proposal through.' She began fidgeting with the material of her skirt as she stared into her lap.

'You have no time to think, nor daydream. A girl often has nerves and misgivings about becoming a wife but it is the natural way of things. You will have a lifestyle your father could never provide for us. The duties of a wife . . . the personal duties,' her mother spoke low as if confiding in her and comforting her fears, 'they do not take long when you consider the amount of time you will be wed, and you learn to adapt until age lessens the demand.' Having revealed this wisdom to her daughter, her mood lightened. 'He, James that is, is dining with us tomorrow after dinner; we shall accept his most generous offer and the wedding will be announced immediately. By the end of the month you shall be Mrs Deadman. Now go and change and resign yourself to a more affluent and interesting future than you could ever have envisaged. You cannot stay a child for ever — no one can.' She laughed. 'You might well have one of your own by this time next year and I will be a grandmother.' She looked at Muriel. 'Of course your sister has a head start on you; she will no doubt beat you to that duty, but not to worry. Still, one of you must produce a boy. Oh, how exciting it will be to see which of my girls is the first to have an heir of their own,' she said, and had to stop for breath as she had become so excited and flustered by her own ideas. 'Both married to men of rank! I never thought it possible. Our future will be far better than we have ever known, you'll see.'

Molly left the room with Muriel, who had looked a little sheepish when her mother had mentioned her having a child.

'Are you already with child, Muriel?' Molly asked as they stepped into the hall.

Muriel flushed. 'I'm not sure. Perhaps, sometimes these things take time and we have only been married six months, Molly.'

'Muriel, are things 'well' between you and Philip?' Molly asked quietly.

Her sister rounded on her in a waspish voice. 'Do not ask things about which you have no knowledge, Molly. Things are quite 'well' between us, thank you!' She stormed off up the stairs.

Molly watched her go, knowing for certain that all was not well between them and hoped for her sister's sake that they would sort out their differences. There was a time when Muriel would confide in her, but then she had married and Muriel became a lady in the growing town. She no longer needed her childish sister. Molly looked longingly at the door; she picked up her pelisse and walked out. If she could have no peace in the house she would stay outside.

Nearly an hour later she had left the town and climbed up a low hill on a path that led into woodland. The path was obviously a track between villages. It was well worn. She looked up at the sky. Even that had lost its sparkle. Cloud had moved across and the sky, instead of spreading sunshine, was now grey and darkening at an alarming rate. So deep in thought, Molly had lost track of both time and distance. She looked down at the village and realised that the impending gloom was not only in her mind, but in the weather. She saw the storm brewing before she had the chance to run back. The first few drops of rain were sporadic, and then the deluge started. She had tried to run down the path, but the water poured from the sky at such a rate that within moments her skirts were heavy with it, her back was soaked through as the rain ran off her spencer, and she had to take shelter.

The noise of thunder as it crashed overhead hid the sound of the horse's hooves approaching along the path behind her.

She almost screamed when the first she was aware of Dr Russell Deadman was when he leaned down from his horse and shouted something to her about placing her foot in the stirrup. He had taken his boot out of one and was holding his arm out for her to grab. She did not know what to do. He swung his other leg over the saddle and slipped down. Both of them were soaked through, only the horse acted as if there was nothing wrong. Without further comment he took hold of her by the waist, a hand either side, and lifted her up. She could feel his strength through the wet cloth of her dress.

'Swing your leg across its saddle and sit upon it like a man.' Her skirts hung heavy and were in the way. He pulled the fabric up, placed her on the saddle then climbed up behind her.

Molly was beyond embarrassment. Her sister's bonnet was ruined. The velvet spencer sagged and drooped in an ungainly fashion like an old cloth, and her pretty dress was clinging to her or bundled up by her knees, revealing her calf and her boots. Her hair hung lank. She was a mess. He did not stop. Before she knew what was happening or where he was taking her they travelled at speed, beyond a trot, into a canter and then to a gallop as he headed away from the town to an outlying house. Molly found that, despite the conditions, she was smiling as she felt the animal move beneath her. Dr Deadman had an arm around her, holding her firmly so she felt safe. It was another new and exciting experience.

He rode straight to the door of the grey stone building and slipped off the back of the horse. He then lifted her down.

'Stay there a moment.' He left her standing in the shade of a small porch whilst he disappeared around the back with the horse. Some moments later he came back, soaked to the skin, and led her into the house.

There was no sign of any servants. In the hallway she dripped onto the tiled floor. He peeled the spencer off her and dropped it in a soggy heap near the door. Her dress clung to her body. She felt almost naked before him. He ran up the stairs and returned quickly with blankets.

'Come with me.' He led her down a corridor to the back of the house where there was a large fire burning in the kitchen. 'There is nothing to worry about. Cook will not return for four hours, that is, if the weather improves. Meanwhile, take off your wet things and wrap yourself in the blanket. We must get dry.' Without further ado he stripped off his shirt and pulled the blanket around him. He had turned his back to her and she could see clearly the marks from a flogging. She was stunned.

He carried on removing his boots and then his breeches dropped to the floor. He was very discreet and wrapped the blanket around himself rubbing his body dry. Without looking at her he calmly said. 'If you do not do likewise you will become very ill. I will have to remove the garments for you, as a doctor and a friend.'

Molly turned her back and was soon wrapped in her blanket, standing next to the fire. He picked up her clothes which he arranged over a laundry rack by the fire.

'Now who looks like a frightened rabbit?' he said, and grinned. She could see a family resemblance to James. 'We shall now go up to my bedroom and sort out some attire for you to wear.'

'I do not think so!' she snapped.

'Then stay here on your own and I shall dress. However, if anyone does come in you might frighten them with your current appearance.' He left the room.

Molly stared at the fire for a few

moments but then felt so uncomfortable in her state of undress that she followed him up the stairs.

'Were you looking for me? Did you follow me, sir?' she asked as she caught up with him.

'No, I have better things to do than that. Binton, who is a tenant on the estate needed my help, or rather his wife did. I delivered her a fine boy this morning. I was on my way back to see James when I saw you run for cover in the woods.'

'Why do you want to talk to James? Are you going to threaten him again?'

He laughed. 'No, he summoned me. He must feel he has some news for me. Has he?'

'How should I know?' Molly said, as they stopped outside what was obviously his bedchamber.

'How indeed!' he commented drily and walked in. Molly hesitated in the doorway. 'Find anything that you will feel warm and comfortable in.' He pulled open some drawers and selected his own attire. 'Please, I shall be next door dressing. I shall cough loudly before re-entering. Then you must let down that hair and we shall dry it by the library fire. Then perhaps we may be able to talk without bickering and you may yet learn to trust me — just a little.' He left her alone staring at his bed and drawers. What was becoming of her life? This was all wrong. One man kissed her by the river then the other invites her, in a near naked state, to share his clothes. If only her father knew!

9

Molly felt very guilty as she carefully rummaged through Russell's clothes. She pulled out a shirt and a waistcoat, a pair of his breeches and quickly dressed. She was holding the breeches up in one hand, realising a belt was needed. She opened another drawer and pulled on what she thought was a leather belt which was, in fact, attached to a length of braid. She moved it towards her to reveal a cavalry sword, highly polished which lay across a carefully folded uniform.

She heard Russell cough and quickly pushed the drawer closed. When she turned around, still hanging onto the breeches which were overhung by the ample shirt and waistcoat, she had the look of childish guilt written across her face.

He leaned against the door frame.

'You look a sight.' He was grinning from ear to ear.

'You said to dress in your clothes. I did but they are too big so I was looking for a belt.' She held her head high, which matched the colour in her cheeks.

'And you found my sword and uniform,' he commented.

She blushed even deeper, feeling guilty as if she had trespassed upon his private life — one hidden away from the world. She was also aware of the situation she was in. Standing in a man's clothes in his bedchamber in an empty house — empty of servants that is.

'So why look so guilt ridden. If I had meant to keep it a secret I would not let you loose amongst my personal things, would I?' He walked into the room, opened the drawer, removed the sword and showed it to her.

'You were in the wars . . . fighting the French?' Even to her own ears her voice sounded incredulous.

'Why are you so surprised?' He replaced the weapon and instead took out a belt from another drawer.

'It is just that you have been flogged, and I wondered if that was why you are not serving in the war anymore.'

He spun around and laughed as if he did not believe the notion that had crossed her mind. 'You think that was done as a punishment of some kind, by my own side?' He shook his head. 'No, lady, my sword was not broken nor was I drummed out of my regiment. The flogging was at the hands of a Frenchman who had taken a dislike to me, despite my rank. He should have honoured the parley, but instead he took his pound of flesh first. He sought revenge for the defeat of his men. However, it came at a price and I and three other soldiers paid it. I survived; they who were men from the rank and file did not. War is neither fair nor just, not from the eyes of one who has trained to save lives.'

'Oh, so you are not a cowa . . . ' She

cut her comment dead as she realised what a foolish and insulting thing she was about to say.

He laughed at her. 'I see that you have indeed met James, Molly. No doubt he has told you I am a bitter man and jealous of his every gift. He is nothing if not predictable; the emphasis being on 'he is nothing'.'

She raised her eyebrows at his sarcasm.

'I suppose he has also wooed you and now you too are in love with his carefree attitude and wild promises. Do you realise you are not the first. However, fortune, if it can be called that, smiles on your union because at least now he actually wants a wife and not just a conquest.'

There was a coldness to his eyes, which changed his whole persona, as if a protective shield had been created. 'Are you sure you are not jealous or bitter, because, sir, your words sound that way?'

He stepped forward and whilst she

held the breeches up he wrapped a belt around her small waist and tied it as best he could so that they would stay in place. She let the shirt hang down over her. Despite the turn in the conversation he still smiled at the sight of her.

Dr Deadman looked at her hair and removed the pins which kept it up even in its bedraggled state. Raven, wet ringlets hung down. He disappeared back into the smaller room and returned with a white towel which he wrapped around her hair and twisted it up as if in a turban style, tucking the end in so that it stayed in place. Then Russell stepped back and nodded.

'A fine creation, even though I say so myself.' Next he picked up a pair of slippers and placed them by her feet. They were crimson, embroidered in gold and very large for her but she slipped them on and laughed as she caught sight of herself in the looking glass. 'My father would want to flog you himself if he could see me here, like this.'

'He has no room to stand on any moral high ground.' His answer was abrupt.

Her face lost its humour. 'He would still care that his daughter was in a vulnerable and dishonourable position.'

'Yet he would match you with a gambler, a lush and a womaniser.' He shook his head. 'You have my sympathy.'

'What has he ever done to you that you would besmirch his good name so? Did the love of your life really take a shine to him?' Molly thought if they were to be so candid, she would seek out the truth.

He walked to the door. 'Come with me to the library and we shall dry that hair before I end up caring for you in a professional way.'

'I think my question deserves an answer,' she persisted as she flip-flopped her way after him.

'He is not for you. He is a wastrel and a cad. So his summons for me to meet him will be for him to offer a threat to destroy my good name and reputation, lest I back off and leave him to catch his prey. He will seek to destroy my credibility and hound me from the town if I do not give my blessing to this match.' Russell made his way down the stairs to the library.

Molly followed as quickly as she could.

'Why does he need your blessing?' she asked.

'Because without it, he cannot afford a wife. Molly, I shall not give it.'

He stepped back and let her walk into a room lined with books on three walls. A fire burned in the hearth. He gestured she should sit by the armchair and towel dry her hair in front of it. She did, just as she would have done at home.

'I thought we were friends. You owe me . . .'

'I owe it to you not to slight you as you are not the gold-digger I thought you to be. You are an innocent pawn in this. However, I will not let him destroy you as he has done others.' He was quite vexed. 'Does your mother know where you went walking?'

'I decided to take the air. I did not actually tell anybody that I was going out. I needed to think.' She looked around her, realising her actions had indeed been rash and a little selfish.

He laughed, looking down at her. 'Did you not think how they might be beside themselves wondering where you have taken yourself off to in the storm?'

'There was no storm when I left.' Her voice was indignant, but she kept her head hanging down because she knew that, through no fault of her own, she had once again found herself in the centre of a situation. Her mother and Muriel would be panicking. If they knew where she was and how she was attired, they would do so even more.

'I think as soon as the weather breaks I will ride over to the house and inform them that you are safe and ask for a change of clothes for you. Yours will not be dry by nightfall.' He turned around, scratching his head. 'You will have to stay here until I return and then I shall see you home safely.'

'Did he tell the truth about your fiancée, sir?' Molly peered through the tendrils of her hair and saw him look down at her.

'The weather has broken sufficiently, I will leave now. Dry yourself. I shall return soon with your fresh attire. Do not let anyone in until I do — especially James. He is no gentleman and you are naive and vulnerable.'

She saw him leave. She could not stop herself from thinking James was right; he was still very bitter about his lost love.

10

'Mother, Molly has gone. She has not been in her room. The maid saw her leave over an hour ago, and look at the weather.' Muriel was almost frantic as the storm had been violent in nature. There was nothing to be done but wait and see if Philip returned home before Molly did.

'That stupid, girl,' her mother shouted. 'What good is a wife if she has pneumonia? Has she no sense at all?'

'She is hot headed, Mother. She hates being told what to do. I don't know what was said between her and Father but neither spoke to each other after breakfast. I fear she may have displeased him greatly. James took to her but . . . I fear she is not ready to be a . . . woman yet.'

Muriel spoke quietly to her mother. The older woman scoffed. 'How old does she need to be?'

Muriel looked away. Her mother ignored her silent plea to talk to her about the subject so dear to her own heart and voice her own worries.

'The time to become a woman and accept our place in life is when we take a husband, for better or worse. We make of it the best we can and that silly girl is going to mess up her chance to net herself a decent catch. So selfish! As for your father, if she thinks she knows more about him and his ways than I do, she is fooling only herself. I welcome his ways, they leave me free to see you and spend time here, in a proper town, in a growing community, whilst he hovers in inns.' Her mother's face looked set in stone as she pursed her lips.

Muriel did not understand the full meaning of her mother's words but she was surprised at the bitterness, almost coldness, with which they were spoken. She was seated in silence by the fire for some time after, when her mother announced the storm had ceased.

'I could send the maid out. She could ask if anyone has seen her,' Muriel said absently.

'What, and have people talk? No, we must wait until the little madam returns or is brought back to us. This really is so like her!' Her mother resumed staring out of the window.

★ ★ ★

Russell Deadman rode into the town. He had deliberately avoided seeking out James, knowing he had missed his summons and determined the man would not know of Molly's whereabouts, and her current situation. He rode straight for the Trentons' house.

'Mrs Trenton, Dr Deadman is here to see you.' The maid looked rather sheepish as her announcement met with yet another waspish comment from her mistress's mother.

'What does he want?'

He cleared his throat before stepping

inside the room.

'Excuse me, ma'am, I have news of Miss Millicent. The lady was caught out in the storm and took quite a soaking. She requires a change of attire.' He looked from one woman to the other with what hoped would be a pleasant expression upon his face.

'Is she well, sir?' Muriel asked.

'Perfectly,' he answered reassuringly, and noticed her mother's eyes narrow.

'Where is she, man?'

Muriel looked anxious at her mother's tone, which was far from gracious.

'She is in my home, ma'am, safe and dry, but in need of fresh clothes to wear so that she may return here. If you could gather some together I will make sure she is here before nightfall. Otherwise, she would be unable to travel.' He looked from one stunned face to the other.

'And what 'state' is my daughter in now?'

'A dry and warm one, ma'am. I am a man of medicine. I made sure she is dry, warm and safe, ma'am. The clothes please, time is passing and I am a busy man.' His manner also changed.

Prudence nodded to Muriel who almost ran from the room.

'Sir, I know you have little respect for my family, but please do not seek to destroy my impetuous young daughter's reputation by taking advantage of this unusual situation. I will send Muriel back with you. Lieutenant Deadman has no need to hear about this unfortunate incident. I'm sure your intentions are honourable.'

'No, ma'am, you will not send Muriel back with me, unless she has a horse to ride upon, because I have ridden here. I will bring Miss Millicent back in my gig when the weather has cleared completely. I am not in the habit of picking on helpless young girls; I leave that to my cousin, Lieutenant James Deadman.'

'How dare you, sir!' Prudence breathed in deeply.

'Easily, for you do not know the man

as I do and you know even less about me. I will take the clothes back and restore your daughter to you. Do not infer anything which would damage my professional reputation, I am warning you on that. I will not have people bandy insults with me when it comes to my professional status. Think what you may of me as a person but do not say it in the company of others. She is safe and perfectly unharmed.'

Muriel entered the room with a neatly tied bundle which she handed to Russell.

'Thank you, I will return her before nightfall. Good day.'

'Nightfall!' Prudence Platt repeated.

'Yes, she will need to dine first. Good day.' He walked out.

'Insolent man!' she snapped. 'You wait till I see that fool of a sister of yours, Muriel. What ever did I do to deserve such a foolish child?'

★　★　★

Russell arrived back at the house knowing that his guest was one guardian angel who desperately needed protecting herself. She had a harridan of a mother, a waster of a father and a cad for a suitor. He smiled as he looked at the bundle. She had an appetite for life and a knack of finding herself at odds with it.

He let himself in and found her curled up in his chair apparently reading one of his books, or at least looking at the diagrams. She looked completely absorbed as she studied it and was not instantly aware of his presence. When she saw him she closed the book and smiled. He paused for a moment as her hair, now dry, hung loose over her shoulders. She was beautiful. He had wanted to stop James marrying her, and he still did, but now his motives were more personal. This brought old feelings, long buried, back into play. He would need to take care. James played and toyed with people's emotions. He would not let him see his weakness this time. Somehow he would let Molly know just what a cad James was, and then by comparison what a catch he would be. But how? That was the question he would have to answer quickly as James was in a rush and so were Molly's parents. He, however, would like time to court and know this lady.

★ ★ ★

'I thought you would be longer than that. Did you put their minds at rest?' she asked calmly.

'I told them where you were and that I would return you before nightfall.'

Molly's jaw dropped open. 'You didn't, did you? Mother will be furious. I'd better dress and walk back.'

'No, it's wet out there. You dress and I shall take you home after we have eaten. I think that after your excitement and before you face your mother again you will need sustenance inside you. I shall take you back in the gig later.

Dress in here. I'll sort out the food. I'm sure cook will have left something for me to eat.'

He left the room and closed the doors behind him.

Molly looked at the bundle of clothes. She knew she was in trouble again, but somehow the thought of staying a while longer pleased her. She set to dressing herself by the warmth of the fire, wondering if it were possible for her to bridge the gap between these two estranged cousins. Perhaps, she thought, she was the person who could help Russell to see just how gentle James could be.

Once dressed, she made her way to the kitchen. There was a pleasant aroma leading her to it. She walked in, not expecting to find anyone but Dr Deadman there.

A feminine voice took her by surprise. 'Now where would you be going, miss?' She turned around to see a woman holding a jug of milk in her hand coming out of a larder.

'I was looking for Dr Deadman,' Molly replied lamely.

The woman put her head on one side, looking at her curiously. 'Tell me.' She walked her into a room which was clearly for laundry. Her soaking garments had been hung high on drying racks, including the velvet spencer. 'Would they be yours?'

Molly nearly said no, they were actually her sister's, but she realised that would not sound right either. 'Why yes, I was out when the storm broke. Where is Dr Deadman?'

'He will be in his day room. Dinner will be ready in half an hour, miss. If you go back to the hallway it is the door opposite the library. He won't like it if he thinks you've been where the servants go. So you best return to wherever he last left you before George comes in. He's Dr Deadman's manservant. He's been given the day off as his brother's bairn was delivered this morning. Good day for it, eh? What an omen to come into this world in such a storm. Still, miss, you best return before you're missed. If them clothes up there are yours, wherever did you get those clothes from that you are wearing now, miss?'

'Dr Deadman went to my sister's home to collect them. I was very wet.' She was feeling uneasy.

'So what was you wearing whilst he did that?'

'There you are!' Dr Deadman's voice resounded down the hall. Instantly, Cook started about her business. 'I hope dinner will not be long.'

'No, sir, not at all. I was just showing the young lady that her things were fine.' She bobbed a curtsey to both of them and scurried off to the kitchen.

'Come with me.' He walked her back to the room where the cook had said he would be waiting for her. It had a small table set for two by the window. The room itself was furnished in rich fabrics. There was not a book in sight here, but a small stove kept the room warm. He saw her looking at it. 'I do not want to waste the heat. This warms here and the heat keeps my room upstairs warm also. I am gradually improving the house.' He gestured that she should sit down on one of the comfy sofas. He then sat on the edge of it and turned sideways to face her. 'You should never have to explain yourself to a servant. Do not give them information which could be retold and in turn damage your own reputation. Cook is excellent at her job, but she is neither your, nor my, keeper. Do not empower her by confirming or compounding her knowledge. You are my guest and that is good enough for her to know. By talking with her you have already told her you are not used to having a servant.'

'I was looking for you,' Molly tried to explain.

'Exactly my point.'

'I am not used to servants.' Molly looked defiantly at him.

'She does not need to know this. You are my guest, therefore you behave as a lady would.'

Molly leaned back. 'Are you reproving me, sir?'

'No, just giving you some sound advice. It may come in useful in your future.'

'Really, so if I am your guest, I am no longer good enough as Molly Platt. Who should I try and be then, Lady Millicent?' She folded her arms.

He sighed. 'With me you are Molly, and to them you can be Miss Millicent, my guest, if you wish. It is you who I am trying to protect, not I. You look childish when you do that.' He pointed to her arms.

'That's what I mean, 'not I', why not 'not me'. Muriel carries off this sort of thing far better than me — or 'I'.' Molly placed her hands into her lap.

'So if you become a wife, does it bother you that you may enter a level of society who will never accept you?'

'You mean as a lieutenant's wife?' she asked pointedly.

'Possibly.' He was considering her closely.

She leaned forward, her face close to his. 'You would even use this to try to dissuade me. He would be at war. You tell me that army wives are still worried about frippery and manners when their men are fighting a war?'

'Yes, more so in some cases, as they cling to what gives them peace of mind, threads of their life at home. It is a far bleaker existence for the wives of the common soldier who follow their men and exist in dirt and rags, many to find themselves scraping an existence when they lose their man.'

She could not answer him, for he knew the truth of that from what he had heard her father tell her mother.

There was a noise outside the door as their dinner was brought. 'Come, forget this conversation and let us prepare to eat.'

He took Molly by her hand and led her to a seat at the table. The silver cutlery and pretty plates were so different to the pewter plates of home. She sat down as Cook entered.

'Excuse me, sir, but George has not returned yet.'

'Never mind that, Johnson. Tell him he will not be required again today when he eventually strolls in. I am well aware he will have been wetting the baby's head with his brother.'

The woman set down two bowls of soup and some fresh bread on the table, placing each bowl in front of them. 'The mutton will be ready when you are, sir.' She left them alone, closing the door behind her as she went back out.

'It is lovely,' Molly said, as she sipped her way through her portion.

'I have never truly thanked you, Molly, for rescuing me. I did a very foolish thing by going there and asking questions about your father. You realise what their reaction meant, though, don't you?'

Molly put down her spoon wondering how she would manage the mutton after eating so much. She saw Russell's eyes staring at hers, concern obvious again. He really was too serious for his own good.

'Yes, they didn't like you asking questions about locals.' She was sipping the glass of wine which was on the table. Molly hadn't realised it was for her until she saw him drink his. She was not used to drinking wine, but it did taste delicious. She twirled the glass gently with her fingers as she replaced it on the table. He placed his hand over hers and stopped her.

His touch made her focus upon him again. It was more confident than James' eager embrace. She flushed a little at the memory.

'It means they did not like me asking questions about Solomon Platt. They immediately presumed I was from the revenue. Why? Perhaps because in some way your father is in or was in league with their exploits.' He had removed her fingers from the glass and was holding them in his fingers.

She looked at them. His hand was not that of a man used to hard toil but one who this very morning had brought a life into the world. How at odds they were — one cousin sent out to kill an enemy as a soldier and one to save lives at home. She thought about what he was saying to her and realised his meaning.

'You think my father is part of a smuggling network, yet you let him go, why?' she asked, without removing her hand.

'Because of you. I think you may have saved my life. If I destroyed him, I would also destroy your world and that of your sister's, and Trenton. I have spoken to him and he will be setting your father straight. Did you know he was involved? You do not appear to be shocked by this news.'

'After what I have learned about my father's behaviour, it would not surprise me. Army men, who return injured to our shores, do not usually provide well for a family. Even if Philip was helping, we have not been hungry once in my memory; although we do not dine like this.'

Cook opened the door and Russell

slipped his hand from hers to his glass. If Cook saw, she gave no sign of it. A few moments more and the smell of cooked mutton drifted in as their meals were placed in front of them.

'Molly, you do not need to marry James in order to escape from your mother and father's grip.' His words were spoken slowly as if he was trying to say something, yet was uncertain as to how best to phrase it.

Molly stopped eating for a moment. 'Yes, I do. I have insulted my father; my mother is frustrated with me and if I do not marry I risk a life of torment. However, if I do they will be happy, I will be free to leave and you will ruin my sister's life and Philip's future. I am in an unenviable position am I not?' She smiled cheekily at him.

He smiled at her. 'When you put it like that I suppose it does sound grim. Then I shall give you a third alternative. Come and live here with me. I need someone to help me whip this house into shape and who will work alongside me, share a vocation. Someone who is practical, as opposed to prissy and not obsessed by fashion. I can show you London, Harrogate and York . . . '

The fork which was half way to her mouth stopped. Slowly she replaced it onto her plate. 'You are asking me to live here and work with you . . . for you . . . along with George and Cook? This is your alternative, your magnanimous offer to solve the problem?'

He nodded with enthusiasm. 'Yes, Molly, I think you would be perfect. Of course you would have to sit in on a few of my patients first to make sure you had the stomach for it, but I'm sure you would. The way you rallied to my aid shows me that you have grit and that is what is needed. I will deal with the family. They will not question my will.' His usual reserve had left him. He was all animation, lost to his grand plan, unaware that she was staring at him. He had tossed her engagement offer aside and replaced it with, what to her seemed to be the offer of a position some way between housekeeper and nurse.

He was stopped in his reverie when Lieutenant Deadman burst into the house and then into their room.

'James!' Molly exclaimed.

They were eating by a window, lit up for all to see; it was not hard for him to go straight to them.

'When you missed our appointment I should have known why. What lies has he told you, my dear Millicent?' He strode over to the table and placed a protective arm around her shoulder. Russell sat back, and slammed his napkin down on the table.

'I do not believe he has told me any. I was caught out in the storm and Dr Deadman kindly took me in.'

'How very gallant of you,' James snapped.

'You two should be friends,' Molly said casually as the two men glared at each other with mutual loathing.

'I have a gig outside; your mother is beside herself with worry. It is time you returned home.' He picked up the empty wine glass of Molly's and placed it back down. 'Even I would not have imagined that you would sink so low as to try to inebriate Miss Platt.'

'Careful, James, don't overplay your hand or I will call you out, right here and now!'

James laughed. 'I can see you have had a merry time of it. Such bravado is hardly necessary. Come, Miss Millicent, I will see you home safely, at your own mother's request. It is time you left.'

Russell stood up. 'You do not have to go. Stay.'

Molly stood also; her head felt peculiarly light. James' hand cupped her arm. 'I think I must. However, thank you for your kindness and compliment Cook on her excellent food.'

'Think over carefully what I have said, miss,' Russell said as he reluctantly saw them out. Molly was aware of James glaring at Russell as he spoke.

The night air hit her hard as she

climbed into the gig. She had not realised just how tired she was. It had been a very unusual day. As they made their way down the drive, James wrapped an arm around her and pulled her into his warmth.

'What was it you are to think over, Millicent?'

'Oh, I think he wants a housekeeper, he offered me the chance to apply.'

James laughed, his mood was infectious. 'That man is priceless. He has no understanding of a woman's heart at all. No wonder Lydia left him so easily.'

'Who is Lydia . . . was that the name of his fiancée?'

'Who. Oh yes. It's all in the past now.'

'What happened to her?'

'I heard she married,' he said casually and shrugged his shoulders. 'Once she realised I did not feel for her the way she did for me, she looked elsewhere. I think I actually did him a favour by showing him what she was really like. He will never see it, so we must leave him where he is, locked in the past, whilst we, my dear, plan for our future.'

He slowed the gig down before they entered town and turned his face to hers, kissing her tenderly on her lips. She neither pulled away nor met his enthusiasm. 'You will be more than any housekeeper to me, dear Millicent.'

Molly felt warm, she suspected as much from the effect of the wine as from James' words, but she found comfort in his embrace and wondered if she could really trust James' silver tongue. No, she thought, as he straightened up once more, obviously pleased that he had her attention and her heart. His tongue was like liquid gold. It painted a picture of a perfect caring beau. If she were completely naive she would hang on his every word, take succour from his every fleeting touch and long for his next kiss. Instead, she found herself asking questions?

He stopped the gig outside her sister's home. As the door opened, Molly prepared herself for a tirade from her mother once she had been safely delivered by James. They had asked him to stay but he said he had to report back and he would see them at dinner.

Molly ran to her room, ignoring her mother and sister, and took herself off to bed. Within a day her mother would announce the engagement to the world. How sober she felt now. For no reason she could fathom she knew in her heart she did not want to marry James, but neither did she want to settle as Dr Deadman's housekeeper, but why? It offered her a way out and a chance to do something in her own right. She thought back to him holding the belt, taking her hand, and realised whose touch it was she longed for.

She buried her face into her pillow and groaned. 'What a mess!'

11

Molly dressed and went downstairs quite early, knowing that Muriel and her mother would not arise until a more fashionable hour. They were adapting to the habits of their new life of comparative leisure easily compared with their previous ways in the cottage.

Despite not feeling in the slightest hungry Molly decided she had better eat something before facing her mother again. She had avoided a confrontation with her on arriving home with James the previous evening. The woman had almost cooed over her in front of James, heaping thanks and gratitude upon him for intervening and saving her daughter's virtue. It had all been too much, so embarrassing and presumptive of her, for Molly to stay and listen. James had winked at her discreetly, finding it the best of possible outcomes for him. He was a hero for saving her from what . . . ? Finishing her dinner and finding out precisely what it was that Russell wanted or expected of her?

James had assured her mother that Molly's reputation had not been tarnished and their engagement would be announced soon. He was certain all would be well. Before the birth of the new month they would be making their way to London and from there on to the Continent. Life would never be the same for her again.

Molly was certain it was not going to be.

Philip was about to leave the house. 'Good morning, sir,' she said sweetly to him, as he joined her in the hallway.

He looked at her and half smiled. 'Is it really 'good', young Miss Molls?'

She giggled, as it was a stupid pet name which he had only used a few times away from the ears of her family who would have disapproved of the familiarity. He treated her like a young sister, though, so there was no harm in it that she could see.

'You seem to have a gift for the opposite. Chaos follows in your wake. My usually calm house turns into a circus, a sleepy town spins on its heels with gossip as they try to figure out, *which Deadman has the Platt girl got her talons in?*' and my life becomes bothersome. I wonder if, instead of being in the militia I should fight the French for a rest.'

'It is not intentional, sir. Things just happen to me.' She glanced at herself in the looking glass and decided in a second that she would have to do.

'Yes, that is the crux of it. If I thought you were deliberately causing turmoil I would send you to Napoleon directly. Why are you wearing your walking shoes, coat and bonnet?' He folded his arms and stared at her, adopting an authoritive manner.

'I wanted to take the air before Mother arose, so that I would be fresh to speak with her when I tell her of my decision.' She was keeping her voice low so that she did not arouse anyone else in the house.

'Do you actually have a decision left to make, Molly? I thought it was all being planned for you.' He relaxed his posture.

'They can't force me to marry a man I do not want. This is not the middle ages, you know.' She smiled, a little nervously.

'Yes, I realised that as I put my suit of metal armour aside this morning. However, you can be coerced.' He picked up his hat and held it under his arm, glancing at the stairs to make sure that no one else was waking. 'Walk with me a way, talk to me, and tell me what it is that is truly your intention.' He held open the door and she stepped out. The sun was shining again and not a cloud was in sight.

They walked a good few paces before he looked down at her and spoke. 'You have no idea how becoming you are, Molly. If I were still single I think I would cast both Lieutenant and Doctor

Deadman aside and snap you up myself. You have opened up from a dull bud to a beautiful blooming rose who has no idea of her appeal, nor her sensuous aroma, despite those barbs which cause so much bother.'

'Philip, you speak out of turn. You are married to my sister; you should not say such things.' She was watching where she was walking, avoiding eye contact with him, because she was fond of him, but not in love with him. He was Muriel's husband.

'I am only too aware that I married your sister.' His voice had an unusually bitter note.

'Philip, is something not right between you? You chose to marry Muriel, knowing her family and background so why be so harsh on her now?' She did look at him this time as concern for their marriage was real.

'Oh, seeing as it is you I am speaking to and I can at least be honest, I shall tell you something you must never repeat to a soul. Your sister believed herself to be pregnant. Don't look so shocked. I had met her a few times and one day when spirits were too high, the sun was bright, we had spent the day by the river, carefree, laughing and . . . well, I forgot myself. We both did. So I did the honourable thing. I made Muriel my honourable wife and raised her up instead of setting her lower. She was not pregnant.' He stared at his feet as they stood at the corner of a lane.

'She thought she was and could have been. So she did not lie to you. You would have been her ruin if you had not married her, Philip. Besides you were so right together. Why then are you so at odds now?'

'Because she has become so respectable. We had fun, Molls. I was a bit hard on her at first making sure for her own good sake that she knew how to run a home, talk to servants, meet my parents. She learned quickly but Muriel has changed and . . . ' he looked away.

'You want your friend back. That is why she is not pregnant now. Oh, for goodness sake, Philip! Send Mother back to Father and take Muriel back to the river or the beach or wherever you two laughed and 'played' together. She is not happy either. She merely acts her role to please her husband, not to make him miserable.' She laughed. 'And you two think you can help me sort out my mess?'

Lieutenant Trenton blushed and straightened his back. 'Miss Platt, we came to discuss your problem as I recall.'

'I shall not marry James. He is funny and dangerous,' she lifted her eyebrows hoping to infer his appetite for closeness, 'but his tongue trickles golden honey so easily that I cannot be certain what lies behind it. He hardly knows me but professes to be hopelessly in love with me.' She shrugged.

'To be blunt, Molls, he wants you and to have your beauty at his side. He desires you, of that I am sure.'

Molly scoffed.

'You are blind to your own beauty

which adds to its appeal. I think Dr Deadman fell in love with you the moment you rescued him.'

'You know?'

'Your secret is safe, only the three of us know the truth of it. Your father guessed you might have been where you should not but he was not certain.'

'You are wrong, Philip. Dr Deadman is grateful to me. He does not love me in any way. He merely sees me as a practical person who could make him a handy housekeeper.' Molly saw humour in Philip's eyes.

'You are wrong.' His manner was so full of certainty.

'No! You are wrong. He had asked me to work for him last night when James so timely interrupted us.' Molly saw his expression change quite dramatically.

'Molly, enjoy your walk. I must go now. Don't do anything rash until I return before dinner. Appease your mother and Muriel and stay in company when James arrives. Please

take care not to create another storm.'
He made to step away.

'And will you act on what I said about Muriel? I want to see her smile again.'

He winked at her, and coloured a little, as he made his way at speed toward the stable block behind the inn.

12

Molly had not been on her own long when James appeared at her side. It was almost as though he had been waiting for her to appear.

'My day is complete and yet it has only just begun!' He bowed before her, causing a pair of young ladies walking across the street to giggle at his display. He gave them a broad smile and a knowing wink.

'Sir, you must learn how to behave in public.' Molly sounded vexed; it was as much at his presence as his actions. She wanted to be away from him until she had sorted a few things out.

He stood straight, as if he had been brought up on his behaviour by a senior officer; he had been suitably chastised by her. 'You are quite correct. I must keep my eyes fixed only on you and my merriment for when we are quite alone and not in a public place.' He fell into step alongside her and only nodded and greeted people politely as they passed by.

'Lieutenant Deadman I think we should talk honestly to each other, but now is not the time or place, sir.' She was sounding and being stiff. Molly couldn't help it. She had wanted her own company this morning. Philip's conversation and revelations had given her enough to think about on top of her own precarious situation, without him adding to it.

He stopped and looked at her for the first time with a questioning glint in his eyes. She had not seen his confidence dented before. At last he was taking her tone seriously, only he seemed to be planning a new line of attack. Molly wondered if she should just ask him to go away, but decided against it. She was, she decided, being unfair.

'I thought that we had agreed between you and me, we would call each other Millicent and James. Why do

146

I feel a cold draught chilling my side when last night there was a warm heart beating next to mine?' He looked at her with the eyes of a sad puppy.

'You are impossible, James. I just think we are making far reaching decisions too quickly. Everything is so rushed. James, you are older and more worldly than I. I have to be sure.' She had not meant to blurt out her feelings in such a blunt fashion. She had been asked by Philip not to start another storm, yet here she was on the edge of one. Could she steer away from it again to a place of safety and hold it off till he returned this evening? She had hoped to see Dr Deadman this morning. Molly was hoping to walk to his house, daring herself to call there and retrieve her sister's clothes in the hope that he would finish the previous evening's conversation and that they could come to some understanding. After dinner this evening, when she deferred her decision or turned James down outright, she may well need somewhere else to live.

Molly's mind was filled with so many questions she was quite unaware at first that James had carefully steered her down a lane which took them to the river. He had walked her away from people's vision.

'I have explained already, I am in love with you, Millicent. What more can I say or do to impress my sincerity and feelings upon you? I have no time to court you as I would dearly wish to and as you so deserve.' He glanced around them then fell to one knee before her. 'See, I would bow before you in the open. Marry me, my dear Millicent, and do me the honour of being my wife.'

Molly pulled on his shoulders. 'Stand up, James. Do not do this, please. It is so . . .'

'Honest, daring, desperate, sincere . . .'

'Pathetic . . .' Russell's voice brought James instantly to his feet.

'Dr Deadman,' Molly said, as she stared up at him sitting atop his horse.

She noticed the bundle tied onto the back of his saddle and realised that it must be her sister's clothes. Molly smiled as they must have both woken and thought the same thing. They had unfinished business, or at least a conversation.

'You are not wanted here, Russell. This is a private moment between Miss Platt and myself. Remove your nag, and be about your business, whilst I see to mine.' James stood in front of Molly, possessively.

'Gentlemen, I think that you should really try to . . . '

James spun around and glared at her. His mouth curled into a smile, but his eyes were angry. Molly had for the first time glanced behind his usual personable façade. 'Millicent, this is a matter of honour between Russell and me. Please, stand aside and do not interrupt. This is man's business.' He faced Russell once more and failed to see the fire of indignation which now burned in Molly's eyes.

Russell lifted a hand, a silent plea for her to back down. James laughed straight away thinking the gesture was for him and therefore Russell was living up to the image he had painted of him as a coward.

'I think it might be best, miss, if you returned home.' Russell untied the bundle and walked his horse over to where Molly was now standing a few steps away from James. 'They are not completely dry, but they have been laundered. I still have possession of the velvet spencer,' he smiled. 'It will take more work to rescue but Cook informs me it is possible.' He glanced at James and his expression changed again. 'If you would return to your sister's, I will visit shortly.'

Molly nodded and walked back towards the lane.

'Stay here, I will have my answer. This man has interfered in my life for the last time. Millicent, do not let him come between us. It is the power he craves.' He was almost shouting.

Molly shook her head. 'I'm sorry, James, but this is not right. The time and place are not right.' She walked along until she was out of their line of view, ignoring the look of disappointment upon James' face.

Both men's attention firmly focussed upon each other.

'Stay away from her, I am warning you I will not stand by and let you ruin another young woman's life.' Russell stayed upon his horse.

Molly had squeezed against the wall of the last cottage. She could hear the words spoken and could just see the two Deadmans as they squared up to each other.

'You still cannot accept that the love of your life left you so easily, can you, cousin? The lovely Lydia, so well bred, so pretty and so naive and so eager to find happiness in the arms of another. Tell me, if you loved her so much, why did you not take her back as your wife, regardless of what had happened between the two of us? You let her down, Russell, you threw her to the wolves!'

Molly saw the look of pure hatred on Dr Deadman's face, but he did not shout, rant or attack. He walked his horse back a few steps and then turned the horse away riding it off at a steady pace, James openly laughed at him. 'Coward!' he shouted after him.

Molly made her way back to the house. She did not understand either man. James was unkind, she was sure of that; he wallowed in Russell's private pain. However, Dr Deadman had ridden away and not defended his actions. Molly wondered why. Had he simply turned the other cheek? Not rising to James' taunts, or was he as James had insinuated, a coward who did not face up to his cousin. This Lydia seemed a tragic figure. Neither man had helped her, so what had happened to her? Before Molly entered the house she sighed; none of it was of importance to her anyway because when she spoke what was on her mind to her mother, she may well be ruined herself . . . or murdered.

13

Lieutenant Trenton was riding back into the town as Dr Deadman headed out of the lane. He saw him and quickly rode over the bridge to cut him off at the end of the main street.

'Dr Deadman, I have been to your house. I obviously missed you.'

'Is someone hurt?' Russell was distracted. He was still curbing his urge to go back, dismount and give James a thrashing once and for all, but he was trying to stifle it. Why give him the satisfaction. Then he would have the ammunition he needed against him and his profession. He was not so stupid as not to see through the man's guile. He'd willingly take a beating, act the injured party and have Russell's reputation tarnished irreparably as a man not worthy of his profession and trusted place in society. The man simply wasn't worth the instant satisfaction he would have of wiping the smug grin off the cad's face.

'No, sir, not in the way you are meaning.' Trenton began to explain.

'Are you speaking in riddles, man?' Russell asked, as he glanced back to the lane. James had not yet appeared. 'Come for a ride with me and explain yourself.'

Both men cantered out of the town until they were in the open country.

'What is your point, Philip?'

'I wish to speak about my sister-in-law. Her mother is determined to see her wed and James wishes the engagement to be made formal within the day. Molly, Millicent, that is, does not wish it.'

'Then why doesn't Molly say so clearly and have done with the man.' Russell was toying with his reins. He loathed James and hated the way he manipulated people to please his own desires. She was naive; she had a life ahead of her, James would steal it from her and then toss her aside once he was bored. If he was not killed by the French eventually he would either drink or gamble his future away.

'She intends to, but I do not envy her her position. If she returns to the cottage with her mother, her life will be hell. Prudence is not staying beyond the week. I have stomached her long enough. It is time Muriel and I had our home back.'

'How is she hurt . . . ? Has James . . . ?' Russell's grip tightened on the reins.

'No, nothing like that, he has had little enough opportunity. It is you who has hurt her.'

Russell was confused. 'I have not seen her since James burst into my home yesterday evening.'

'As you were asking her to be your housekeeper, you mean.' Trenton continued, 'I know it may be seen as generous from your perspective. I am aware I have married beneath me, or at least that is how my dear mother views it. The fact that father's fortune diminished over the years, leaving me little has escaped her. She still thinks my grandfather's fortune should have netted me a lady of the realm. However, I love my wife and shall not regret my decision. You are in a different situation, Russell, a man of means. You can make your own choices without consequence.'

He stopped and stared at Russell who had been quietly weighing up the man's words.

'I'm making a hash of this. What I am trying to tell you is that I think she is genuinely fond of you and finds the notion of being your housekeeper appealing, yet is unsure if it means you still look down upon her. Don't forget, Muriel is my wife. Molly would be in the same town — one sister as a married woman — one as a servant,' Trenton finished. 'That is why she is hurting; her feelings for you and the situation with James are at conflict within her and time is running out.'

Russell smiled.

'It is no joke, Russell. She is dear to me, do not mock her.'

'I am not. More my own stupidity for I am not gifted with James' way with words. I tend to 'make a hash' of it. I shall go to your house at three and throw all of her mother's plans into disarray. Be prepared for a prickly homecoming, Philip. James is about to lose a battle he should never have pitched in the first place. I may need a little of your help here.'

'Do not pick a fight in my home unless you pay for the damage in full. There are ladies present.' He was grinning, but Russell ignored him. 'Listen to me and do what I say, please.' He gave Philip some money and clear instructions as to what he wanted him to do in the next hour and then rode back towards the town.

* * *

Molly was summoned to the day room where her mother was waiting for her.

'You really must stop walking out on your own. Did you not learn from your mistakes of yesterday? If it was not for James your reputation would lie in tatters.'

'I fear if it were left to James alone I would have no reputation to be proud of; he is singular in his attention.' She sat by the window.

'You are very dismissive of a man who is prepared to raise you up, girl. Your future will be so much better with him. You must hide that pride of yours and still that tongue. He was here this morning whilst you wandered aimlessly. The poor man's heart is almost broken as you trifle with his affections.'

Molly laughed, thinking the man would stoop so low as to woo the mother in order to trap the daughter. Her mother was not at all pleased with her.

'Molly, this man may be as wet as the sea itself, but he is one bloody fish you must not let go. Hook him and keep him!'

'Mother, I'd forgotten what your Ebton voice sounded like, so grand are we here.'

'You insolent little fool! I'll knock that smug smile off your face if you throw this man's offer away. You'll be down gutting fish in the village to pay for our food and be glad of Jeb as a man by the autumn, if you dare turn James aside. Don't think you have the pick of the bunch, miss. You are only being considered because your sister has earned her place here. Your father will not let it lay lightly either.'

'Father has no reason to reprove me of my actions.' Molly watched her mother sit back in the chair.

'You think because you know about his strumpet that you can control him. Is that it? Do you think he will hang his head in shame?'

Molly's eyes widened, shocked that her mother knew about Elsie.

'You have no idea. Did it never occur to you that I was happy for him to go to her whilst I was free to come here?

Lass, he spent many years away from me and fighting — killing men for his country. He came back lame, broken and a bitter man. War can do that to a soul. I didn't want him like that. He found someone who did. We all survive the best we can and you now need to marry, and James is the best offer you will get.'

She stood up and walked over to her daughter. 'Molly, I am not wanting rid of you. I want you to have a good life away from the villagers and your father. You have to be brave as I have to let go. Don't hanker for a childhood which you have outgrown. You have been lucky, lass, to know some freedom and joy along with the toil.'

Molly looked out of the window; she swallowed, wondering how she could reject James now without hurting her mother even more. She had not realised just what her mother had put up with in order to bring her and her sister up with enough knowledge and education to make such matches even possible.

'I don't love him, Mother.'

'You don't need to, Molly; just marry him whilst he loves you. In time you will have children and he will look elsewhere. So long as he provides a good home, food and is kindly with the children, then you will have succeeded.'

A tear ran down Molly's cheek. 'I must freshen up and change.' She stood up and walked over to the door.

'Aye, Molly, you freshen up, wise up and change, because if this heart of yours doesn't harden soon, he will break it, any man would.'

Molly looked at her mother's tired face and ran upstairs. She just didn't want to change. She didn't believe that all men were so selfishly callous.

14

Russell arrived at Lieutenant Trenton's dressed in his finest day suit. He had sent word to his friend that he would make his visit at three o'clock precisely. He was to be expected, and hoped that he could also be present.

Philip had followed his instructions: taken James to the inn, had a drink with him and left him with money to buy more. The man was very happy to agree. Then Philip had informed the ladies that they were expecting a visitor so they were to be dressed at their best and present themselves in the day room. He would not say another word on it as he had duties to see to before he could return. At five minutes to three he managed to make the journey to his house, after having a ticking off from his officer for disappearing again.

Russell arrived almost as soon as

Philip had joined the women in the day room.

All three ladies looked surprised as Dr Russell Deadman was shown into the room by the maid.

'Dr Deadman!' Her mother broke the silence. 'What a surprise.' She stared at Philip, who smiled pleasantly at all.

'Well, Russell, let's not keep the ladies waiting, as I have to return to the barracks soon,' he added as if to stress a point.

'My apologies for this intrusion. I have just been to visit your husband, ma'am.' He looked at Prudence who coloured slightly, obviously expecting an underhand motive for his visit to discredit Molly. 'He is well and . . . '

'He is far from well, sir. He is lame and . . . '

'Precisely, he is injured. I am a man of medicine and, after examining his arm, I believe that he can be helped.'

All eyes were upon him. They had not expected him to talk of the father in such a way.

'His arm requires surgery to correct the botched attempts made in the field of battle. I honestly believe it is possible and I know a man in Edinburgh who would be the best surgeon for the job. He is not some army sawbones but a qualified surgeon, my mentor, in fact.'

Molly watched her mother stand. 'Are you going to suggest that if my daughter gives up James you will help my husband to become an able man again? Is that it?'

'Partially,' he acknowledged.

'You sink too low, sir,' her mother exclaimed, and sat down next to Muriel who took one of the older woman's hands in her own.

'You have, once again, belittled me in my words, ma'am. I will see to your husband's arm at my own expense. I have spoken to him and he has agreed. I have also asked him if he would protest if I should ask for your daughter's hand in marriage. To which he offered no objection.'

Philip laughed. 'Well done, Russell, excellent.'

All eyes turned to Molly.

'You wanted a housekeeper and a nurse.'

'I need both, and a wife of mine would need to be versatile as I do not like to fill my home with servants and strangers. I keep two with me whom I trust. I would like to state, though, that I have never been a rash person. I suggest we have as long an engagement as we need to in order to better acquaint ourselves, and in the meantime you accompany myself and your mother to Edinburgh whilst your father has the operation. Mrs Platt, whilst you attend your husband I could show Millicent the city and explain some of the duties expected of her as my assistant and wife.' He turned to Philip. 'This will take a few months, I envisage.'

Philip could not hide his glee. 'Perhaps, ladies, we should leave Millicent and Russell to talk this over.'

Reluctantly, Molly's mother stood. 'You are a clever man, Dr Deadman, but are you sincere?' she asked.

'Never more so, dear lady.'

'Then you have my blessing also,' she spoke quietly and both acknowledged the truce.

The door shut.

Molly looked at Russell who was shifting his weight from one foot to another.

'You have thought of a very appealing alternative for me. Do you really mean to offer an engagement?'

He stood before her. 'Yes, but it can be as long or as short as we choose it to be.'

'Will you tell me where Lydia is and the truth of her?' Molly watched as his eyes showed sadness for a moment.

'The truth is she was a flirty young woman whose attention I had been flattered by. James arrived wanting another loan for his gambling and I refused it. She had told him that we were to marry knowing James would then chase her. He did, but she hadn't realised what a cad he was. He made her pregnant and she turned to me for help — she wanted me to remove the child from her. I refused. The idea was abhorrent to me. I offered her the money James had asked for so that she could have the child and raise it. She took it. I found out later she used it for a back street doctor to take the unborn baby away. She died as a result. James knew, he even knew what she intended to do, but has since distorted the tale and tried to use it to blackmail me.'

'That is awful,' Molly said. 'You did the right thing, though. You mustn't blame yourself.'

'I don't, he does, because he can never take the blame for his own actions. Molly, can we stop talking about James and Lydia, as it is our future I now wish to discuss.'

Molly smiled, 'Sorry. I needed to know.'

'You do, now.'

'Yes.' She watched his face. A silence grew.

'Well?'

'Yes, I will gladly take your offer.' She smiled at the relief on his face then wrapped her arms around his neck and kissed him.

The next few moments vanished in a second as he caught her in his arms and they were as one. When their embrace ended, they realised that they were standing in front of the window and their celebration had been witnessed by two women watching from across the street. Molly smiled at them and waved as Russell laughed.

'I think whilst we are in Edinburgh you may need lessons in etiquette, my dear.'

'Do you really think so?' she said, watching him and thinking what had happened to Muriel and Philip.

To her surprise he answered straight away, 'No, Molly, stay as you are. Now lets share our news with your family and make arrangements.'

'There is still James to deal with.' She hesitated.

'No, not really, you see he has been drinking in the inn most of the day and is currently being collected by the militia and being prepared to be sent down to horse guards to pick up his orders. He is being recalled. Only he will be travelling without you.'

'Thank you, Russell, you saved my life. He would have crushed my spirit.'

'Then we are truly even. Come, your mother awaits and Edinburgh beckons.' He opened the door for her, but Molly knew this was only the first one of many to a much more meaningful and exciting life.

THE END

We do hope that you have enjoyed reading this large print book.

Did you know that all of our titles are available for purchase?

We publish a wide range of high quality large print books including:
Romances, Mysteries, Classics
General Fiction
Non Fiction and Westerns

Special interest titles available in large print are:
The Little Oxford Dictionary
Music Book, Song Book
Hymn Book, Service Book

Also available from us courtesy of Oxford University Press:
Young Readers' Dictionary
(large print edition)
Young Readers' Thesaurus
(large print edition)

For further information or a free brochure, please contact us at:
Ulverscroft Large Print Books Ltd.,
The Green, Bradgate Road, Anstey,
Leicester, LE7 7FU, England.
Tel: (00 44) **0116 236 4325**
Fax: (00 44) **0116 234 0205**